To Hell
and Back

by
Jay Muirhead

Published by

MELROSE BOOKS

An Imprint of Melrose Press Limited
St Thomas Place, Ely
Cambridgeshire
CB7 4GG, UK
www.melrosebooks.com

FIRST EDITION

Cover designed by Jeremy Kay

ISBN 978-1-906050-76-4

Printed and bound in Great Britain by:
Biddles 24 Rollesby Road, Hardwick Industrial Estate
King's Lynn. Norfolk PE30 4LS

One

Helen sat in the armchair looking at her surroundings. She had everything money could buy, but she was scared and alone, she hated every moment she had to endure in this house, her so-called home. Over and over in her mind she asked the same question: Why me? Helen placed her head against the back of the chair and closed her eyes. She struggled with thoughts of her past as she tried to shut them out of her head.

As a teenager life had been difficult; *she* had been difficult. She could still see that disappointed look on her father's face, when the police had brought her home. Falling in with the wrong crowd, she had lied to her parents and now she had been caught shoplifting.

After that, life became unbearable at times: bullied by the gang she had called her friends, she became isolated and withdrawn, but it was her mother's screams at the sight of her daughter's tortured body which Helen never forgot. The physiatrist had told her parents that self-harming was not unusual in young teenagers but left untreated, it could develop into something less controllable. After that her parents never trusted her and seldom let her out of their sight.

Mark had been her friend; without him she had nothing, and now—

The piercing ring of the telephone made her jump. Dragging herself from the chair, she picked up the receiver; there was caution in her voice as she answered.

"Hello."

"Hi, Mum, listen I need to go to Jennie's after school. I wouldn't ask if Jennie could come to ours." Helen's stomach tightened instantly, panic was rising up inside her like a volcano ready to erupt.

"Louise, please don't do this." She tried to control her fear; she had to think of her daughter.

"Our history project's got to be in at the end of the week." There was an awkward silence before Louise said, "Mum, really, it's important ..." Her voice trailed off in a familiar, pleading whisper, one tinged with hope yet expecting denial.

"Okay, but be home for six. God, please be home for six." The moment the words were out she instantly felt sick – why couldn't she just say no?

"I know, Mum. I love you."

The line went dead before Helen could reply. She glanced out of the window. The late afternoon sun shimmered through the trees and across the flowers. Going outside, she took a deep breath. Feeling the rays of the sun on her face, she closed her eyes and enjoyed the warmth spreading through her. She felt her taut body begin to relax and realised how much her tense muscles ached. The garden was a haven, the only place where she was free to roam. Noticing the weeds creeping through the flower beds, she vigorously set to work, spending the next few hours in the garden.

Helen sighed as she walked through each room of the house making sure that everything was in its right place. It was nearly 6 p.m. and Mark would be home from work in the next hour. "A place for everything and everything in its place," he said to her on more than one occasion. But she knew that, no matter what she did, he would find something wrong. He was never happy and tonight would be no different.

Helen was particularly anxious because Louise wasn't home yet. When Louise was a little girl she had been relatively free to go out and play with other children in the neighbourhood, but once she reached a certain age, Mark had become completely unreasonable. Now he exercised the same control over their daughter as he did over Helen: leaving the house without his permission was strictly forbidden.

One evening at dinner, without provocation, Mark had said, "Helen, these so-called friends of Louise's, I don't like her being with them." His face was dark, his eyes challenging.

"But she needs to be with people her own age."

"I will be the judge of what my daughter needs," Mark said in a cold and calculating voice.

Helen knew she was treading on dangerous ground. Lowering her head so as not to challenge him, she spoke softly. "Please, Mark, I beg you; don't do this, not to Louise."

"Have I not made myself clear? Louise will only see friends that I approve of!"

"Bastard!" she spat at him, she couldn't let him do this, not to Louise. Mark rose to his feet, instantly he was beside her. She could feel his warm breath on the side of her face.

"Maybe so, my love, but this is not a request," he whispered into her ear, as he slowly ran a finger down her cheek. He moved his hand down to the base of her neck and rested his palm flat against her chest, pushing her to the chair. Moving his mouth close to hers, he took possession for a brief moment, smiling at her, and whispered, "Don't cross me, Helen, you know what will happen."

But Louise was becoming a young woman and Helen couldn't stand to see her held captive in their home. So, she endured the threats from Mark and on occasion she took a chance and let Louise slip away to a friend's house. Both mother and daughter knew the consequences if Mark ever found out.

In the beginning Helen had genuinely tried to please him, but now she just went through the motions. Every action, every word – any expressed affection on her part – merely served as an attempt to avoid confrontation. She desperately wanted to leave him, living only for the day when she and Louise could be free. This feeling stood in stark contrast to the tenderness she had once felt for him.

She cherished the memory as *the happiest day of her life*, the day Mark proposed to her. They had been on a picnic; he brought a bottle of champagne.

"Helen, there's something I want to ask you." Mark got down on one knee. Taking her hand he said, "I love you, I want to be with you always. Will you marry me?"

Helen remembered holding her hand to her mouth as her lips trembled, small tears escaping her eyes. Unable to speak, she just nodded her head. Their first year of marriage was good. Helen worked at a Special Needs school and for the first time in her life she felt as though she made a difference, that her efforts at the school actually mattered. The children there were all wonderful and, even though it was hard work, she enjoyed a great sense of fulfilment. It was during this time that Mark's true nature began to emerge.

"What do you mean we can't go out on Saturday afternoon?"

"Sweetheart, remember, I'm going on a school trip with the children."

"Yes, the bloody children. Let's not forget the children. Since when do you work a Saturday?"

"Please, Mark, it's my job. We can go out another time."

"I'm only your husband, why worry? *Let's remember the children.*" His voice reeked of sarcasm.

"Mark …"

"Well, you're only a classroom assistant. Why do you have to go? Isn't that the parents' job?"

"They'll be there too. I told you about this trip weeks ago."

"Do you have to mix with these kinds of people?"

"Mark! They're the parents."

"Are the fathers going on this so-called trip?"

"One or two, why?"

"Nice to see the men taking an interest in their children, or is it the classroom assistant?"

"You're being ridiculous."

"Really?"

"Yes, really!" she shouted, unable to hold back tears.

Mark wrapped his arms around her and said, "Please don't cry."

"Why are you being like this?"

"Helen, forgive me, please. I'm just worried that these people are taking advantage of you. Please go on your trip."

"Are you sure?"

"Yes, it's just that I love you and I don't want to lose you."

Helen thought it sweet at first, how Mark seemed so protective. But the occasional twinge of insecurity developed into something else, it escalated. He changed. The more their relationship developed, the more Helen realized that what he really wanted was to control her life. Mark insisted they start a family straightaway. What had begun as a subtle suggestion soon became an adamant demand.

"Helen, what kind of message do you think you're sending when you say you don't want to have my child?"

"Can't we wait a while, Mark? Have some time together first, do other things?"

"Just tell me what's wrong. Is it that you don't love me? Don't you want my child?"

"Mark, love, I didn't say that, not at all. It's just, I really believe if I continue working hard at the school that I'll have a good chance at a promotion."

As soon as she said it she saw the change come across his face, something dark, and with a low voice he said, "You've got the rest of the week to work out your notice and then, Helen, you'll have plenty of time to work out your priorities."

"That's unfair, Mark. No! I won't give up my job!"

"What do you mean, *no*?"

Helen didn't reply. His tight grip on her shoulder said it all. She felt a twinge of apprehension at this new man, a husband she didn't recognise as her own loving Mark.

"Think it through, you know I'm right." There was to be no more discussion.

Less than a year later she gave birth to Louise, and even though she would have preferred to wait a while before starting a family, she welcomed motherhood with open arms. She even managed to convince herself that having a baby would ease the tension in their relationship, prove to Mark that she was a devoted wife. Unfortunately, that dream was quickly dispelled. If anything the new baby solidified his obsessions.

Helen adored Louise. In fact, that was the one part of her life for which she harboured no misgivings, no regrets. But nonetheless, this was what Helen's life amounted to – tolerating an abusive marriage and scurrying about the house in a mad dash to make sure everything was in order.

Helen noticed one of the cushions on the couch was not in the right place. She grabbed it and, out of sheer frustration, shook it hard. She hugged the cushion to her chest. The tears came slowly as bitter reality took hold of her. She existed only for Mark's pleasure, keeping house for a man she no longer loved.

When Mark first bought the house, a surprise wedding gift, it seemed like a dream come true. She worked hard to make it a home, always trying to live up to Mark's high expectations, always trying to be the perfect wife. But nothing was ever good enough, no matter how hard she tried. What, at first, seemed like a dream became a nightmare and the home that once held promise of a good life was now little more than a prison.

Time and time again the same scenes played out. She imagined Mark standing in front of her saying, "Helen, love, if you want anything, just ask me. I will take you if you have a need to go out."

"I know, but I can drive myself."

"I would prefer to take you, wherever you need to go."

"Yes, Mark, but sometimes I like to walk or take the bus."

"A bus? Where might you go on a bus?"

"To see my parents."

"Why must you always be so difficult? You make it so hard to love you. In the future I will take you. It's only because I care, don't you see? I want to do things for you. I want to be there for you, always."

Helen enjoyed living in London. She spent many a pleasant afternoon exploring the street markets. But gradually, even a simple trip to the market became a problem. He asked relentlessly, "What are you trying to prove, Helen? Are you deliberately trying to drive me mad? You're meeting someone, aren't you? Is that it? I'm not enough? Why, Helen? Why am I not enough for you? Why do you do this to me? Don't you love me?" The questions would continue, the cross-examination wouldn't end until she was in tears. He simply wouldn't stop until Helen was full of guilt and remorse, until she was begging forgiveness for imagined crimes. It was always her fault. Endlessly he would tell her, "The only reason I put up with your bad behaviour is because I love you, you belong to me."

Even when Mark knew where she'd be, he showed up using the excuse that he missed her. To all outward appearances it seemed harmless, endearing. He appeared to be an attentive, caring husband. She knew the truth. His anger and jealousy were creations of his own twisted mind, fuelling elaborate fantasies of betrayal. She was left to act out her part, feeling as though she had no choice but to endure this staged version of hell. Mark became more persistent, aggressive and eventually his rage found expression in violence. Enduring the physical pain was one thing; in fact, it seemed almost secondary to the mental anguish she faced – coming to terms with the fact that she was now terrified of a man she had once dearly loved.

She carefully replaced the cushion and sat down on the edge of the couch, her face resting in the palms of her hands. Her stomach was churning and the back of her neck hurt and she was sure she felt another headache on the way. The headaches happened more frequently now and the pain was, at times, unbearable. She took two of the tablets the doctor had prescribed and went upstairs for a quick soak in the tub. It was important she relax before Mark got home. If he sensed even the slightest tension in her demeanour he assumed she was hiding something. He swore he could tell when she had a guilty conscience.

Helen bent over and turned on the taps. As she slowly undressed, she watched herself in the mirror. An immediate sense of guilt washed over her as she stared at the reflection. She knew this woman; she knew that face – she knew it to be her own – but it seemed as if she was intruding on a stranger, watching from a distance as her life went on without her. She was stifled, trapped. She wished she could feel something other than the hatred and fear she had for her husband. She lowered herself into the bath and closed her eyes, trying to imagine a life without him.

Two

Mark ran his hand across the book case: every piece of furniture had been personally selected and paid for by him. He was better than his father, who had been a weak man who gave his wife all the freedom she desired. Mark's mother was nothing more than a whore; all that mattered in her life was other men. Mark gave a disgusted smirk: his parents had neglected him and he would never forgive them. His family would be different, they would be perfect.

For two years after leaving university, Mark and his friend Ian had struggled; their office was in a partially deserted industrial estate. Then, ten years ago, Mark had designed a high-pressure water jet that had the power to cut through steel. Life had changed: he now had a small team of engineers at his disposal.

Making his way across the office, he picked up the phone and dialled. Mark was finding that the last few years of family life had not been as perfect as he thought, but he could always rely on Ian to take the reins when he needed to go home, which was becoming more frequent these days. Ian at least was loyal to him, which was more than he could say for his own wife.

Mark slammed the phone down. Still no answer. He began pacing back and forth, struggling with the images flashing through his mind. He could easily envision Helen in the arms of another man and through clenched teeth he whispered, "In my house, in my bed, my wife. *My wife!* Do they think I'm stupid? Do they think I don't know?"

His jealousy was slowly eating away at him. Vivid thoughts careered through his head. He envisioned Helen responding to another man's touch, groaning with pleasure and desire. He could hear their imagined voices ringing in his ears.

"Kiss me."

"What about your husband?"

"It's you I love, not Mark. Forget him, I do."

"You're beautiful, Helen."

"I'm glad you like what you see."

He imagined *her* seductive laughter, *their* laughter ... ridiculing him as they danced naked together in a wild frenzy of lust and deceit.

Mark loosened his tie. Sweat prickled on his forehead. He felt a horrible sensation deep in the pit of his stomach and the sickening, acidic taste of betrayal welling up in the back of his mouth. He couldn't understand why Helen acted this way. He hated it when she baited him, always flaunting herself in front of other men right before his very eyes, as if he was too thick to notice. He slammed his hand hard against the desk. He was no longer in control. All reason, all logic, took a back seat to his rage. Mark clenched his fists. There was a sharp pain across his knuckles that brought him to his senses. Looking at the hole in the wall he cried, "God, I can't take this any more!" He grabbed his car keys from the desk and walked quickly out of the office. He knew what he had to do. He had to teach her a lesson, once and for all. She had to learn.

When he got to the house he opened the front door and stood still for a moment, greeted only by silence. Where was she? He ran for the stairs, his heart racing, thoughts spinning wildly through his mind.

"God, let her be here," he said, as he took the stairs two at a time, his fear and anger waging war inside his head. "Please let her be alone." He was prepared to face his worst nightmare, prepared to fight for his wife.

When he got to the top of the stairs he stopped and listened. He heard a noise coming from the bathroom. Quietly he opened the door and stepped inside. The sight of her naked body made him smile. She was so beautiful and so desirable and for just a moment he lost himself in the idea of making love to her, caressing her delicate frame, kissing the soft velvety skin of her neck, having her want him like she could want no other, but then rage invaded his thoughts again. He was reminded suddenly why he was there.

"Helen, where were you today when I called?" His voice was calm but there was hatred in his eyes.

"Mark, you scared me!" Helen's senses were immediately flooded with fear and every nerve within her shook. "Give me a minute, love. I'll get out the bath," she said, her voice trembling. She tried to smile at him but it was too late.

The water rushed over her face and her body was pinned against the bottom of the bath. He held her down with no mercy as she struggled. He grabbed a handful of her hair and yanked her head from the water. Helen gasped hysterically for air and with each new breath she gave a desperate scream, pleading with Mark to stop.

"I will ask again. Where were you today when I called?" He gently placed a kiss on her forehead and smiled at her but kept his hand firmly around her throat.

"I wasn't out today, well not out-out, but in the garden. Please! I was in the garden!"

"Ah honey, I love you. Tell me exactly now, what is it to be out or out? Where the fuck were you and who were you with?" He pushed her under again. She was still struggling frantically as he pulled her up.

"Please, I love you! I love you, Mark, nobody else. There's nobody else. Only you." Helen pleaded in between the sobs, but it wasn't enough.

"I won't share you with anyone else! Do you hear me, bitch?"

Her sobs and screams went unnoticed. The water filled her nostrils and mouth again, only this time the blackness came too.

When she opened her eyes again everything was bright, the room was white. She could hear voices. As she tried to sit up, she became aware of something gripping her arm, pulling her back down.

"Helen, love, stay still. You had a nasty fall in the bath." Mark smiled at her. His eyes held a warning and something else, almost a playful cruelty, daring her to speak out. She remained silent.

"Yes, Mrs Waters, listen to your husband. You've given him quite a scare. You're lucky he came home when he did." The nurse gave Mark a toothy, schoolgirl smile. He had charmed this nurse like he charmed everyone else, even her parents thought of him as a caring, loving husband. "I'm going to let the doctor know that your wife is awake," she said, giving Mark another radiant smile before leaving the room.

"Helen, why do you make me do these things? I don't want to hurt you." He took her hand and began caressing it gently.

"I'm sorry, Mark."

"Yes, I know. You're always sorry, but you have to stop telling me lies."

"I know, you're right. Please, I'm sorry."

"Helen, I don't know how much more of this I can take. Why do you keep hurting me this way? What have I done so wrong, that you treat me this way?"

Their conversation was interrupted by the doctor. He made his way to Helen's bedside and took a long look at her chart before he said, "Ah, Mrs Waters, how are you feeling? That's a nasty bump on your head."

"Better now, thanks," she said, managing a weak smile.

"May I take my wife home now?" Mark asked, taking the opportunity to interject the question quickly.

"Well, Mr Waters, we would prefer her to stay. This is the third time in the last two months that your wife has lost consciousness and I would like to run a few tests before we send her home."

"Yes, of course, doctor, whatever you think is best," Mark said, smiling warmly at Helen. "Do you think Helen's condition is serious, doctor?"

"Precautionary measures at this point; don't be alarmed. We're just making sure everything is fine. I note from your chart, Mrs Waters, that you've been experiencing a higher frequency of migraines recently. They certainly can cause unpleasant symptoms such as you've been experiencing – passing out, nausea, sensitivity to light – but we just need to rule a few things out."

"How long will my wife need to stay?"

"No more than two or three days, if that's okay with you, Mrs Waters?"

She didn't say a word – she nodded dutifully, smiled dutifully – but she recognized that the opportunity had come at last, the opportunity she'd been waiting for.

Louise had returned home late from Jennie's just as Helen was being placed in the ambulance. She knew that her father was responsible for her mother's injuries. He always was. Louise played nervously with her hair as she waited patiently. Why hadn't she worked on her project at lunchtime? No, instead she had been selfish and her mum had suffered the consequences. Time passed slowly in the hospital corridor as she waited and hoped for an opportunity to see her. When Louise saw her father coming from a side room, she rushed towards him.

"Dad, is Mum okay? Can I see her?"

"Mum is fine, Louise, just another headache."

"May I go and see her now?" She needed to make sure her mum was okay. She never believed her father, or his excuses as to why these things happened.

"You can have fifteen minutes and not a second longer. I will meet you at the main entrance."

"Yes, Dad, I'll be there."

"You'd better be. I get enough from your mother without tolerating any of your bad behaviour."

She watched him stride away. How she hated him. A "headache"? Didn't he realise that she knew exactly what was going on? Louise entered her mum's room. "Are you okay, Mum?" Her lip trembled, and she felt tears in her eyes. "I'm so sorry I was late."

"Sweetheart don't, this wasn't your fault, okay. I'm fine." Helen smiled at Louise.

"I haven't got long."

"I know. Listen, can you sneak back here tomorrow without Dad? I want to talk to you about leaving home."

"Honestly? Do you mean it?" Louise asked as she held her mother tightly. She squeezed back tears of relief as she dared to imagine it; at last they were going to leave. "Definitely! I'll be here!"

"How long can you stay, love?"

"Just a few minutes, Mum. Dad's waiting for me at the main entrance."

"Okay, you'd better go. Sleep well, Louise, and I'll see you tomorrow."

After Louise had left, Helen lay on the bed staring at the ceiling. She would need to be clear in her mind, if they were to succeed. Carefully she began working through every minute detail; there would be no room for error.

Sneaking out of school the next day, Louise arrived at the hospital shaking with a mixture of fear and excitement. She practically bounced into the hospital room, which did not go unnoticed by her mother.

"Hi, Mum, thought I'd come before lunch," Louise said, trying to sound as casual and normal as possible for her mother's sake. She planted a kiss on Helen's cheek and asked, "How are you feeling?"

"Good. Your father will be here soon, so listen carefully. I've been thinking about the best way to leave your father and we can do it the day I get out of here. I'm going to need your help." She hated the thought of putting Louise in this position but she had no choice.

"How long will you be in here for?"

"Just a few days, I hope, love"

"Can't we just go now?" Louise just couldn't control her excitement.

"Listen to me now, I need you to gather a small amount of your clothes and hide them in my car." Helen kept her eyes firmly fixed on the door; Mark could enter at any time.

"What about money?"

"You've got my bank card, lift what you can, not too much at the one time. God, don't alert him."

"Don't worry, Mum, you can trust me." Louise tried to

sound reassuring. She could see how vulnerable her mother was feeling and, in spite of her brave face, Louise knew with absolute certainty how very terrified Helen really was. She herself knew the same fear. Every time … she felt the pain, not the same as her mother's pain but a tortuous mental anguish just the same. She didn't think her mum really understood that.

"I know I can, love, but don't touch my clothes, he'll notice immediately. Will you remember all of this? I can't write it down, it's too risky." She paused and then said, "Louise, are we doing the right thing? What if he catches us?"

Louise could see her mother's trembling hands. Her eyes were large and fixed as she stared at her daughter, like the eyes of a frightened rabbit caught in the headlights of a car.

"Mum, please, we've wanted this for such a long time."

"I know, but if he finds out, he will kill us. God, I'm so scared."

"Listen to me, if things keep going the way they are he really is going to hurt you. I can't keep watching. Please …"

"I'm sorry, love, it's just that—"

Louise interrupted, "Mum, we can't keep living like this. Please, we have to do this." Panic was welling up inside, her own fears were taking hold but she couldn't let her mum give in now.

"You're right, I'm just being silly. We have to leave for both our sakes," she said, smiling at Louise.

"Is there anything else I can do, Mum?"

"No, you had better go, don't come here too often, and Louise," she said as she reached out to take her daughter's hand.

"Yes, Mum?"

"I love you, be careful."

Louise placed a gentle kiss on her mother's cheek and said, "I love you too, Mum." Without looking back she turned and left. Helen knew that this small action was one of great bravery.

Helen's stomach was churning as Louise left the hospital. She felt sick. What had she done, asking Louise to take such a risk? She was putting her daughter in more danger than ever before. It was the only way that they could escape but it didn't make the guilt any easier to bear. She had to be strong. She deserved, they both deserved, to be free, and all she could do now was wait.

Louise returned to school. Scared of bumping into her father, she kept to the back roads. Since she was a small child, Louise had been aware of her mother's bruises. It wasn't long before she realised that her dad was the cause of them. Often he talked about her mother's indiscretions, that they had to be punished, but Louise knew her mother rarely left the house because she was too scared of Mark. Over the last few years, her dad turned more of his attentions to her, restricting her from friends and activities. Louise had learned never to ask her dad for anything. She also knew that any objections she raised to him would result in her mother paying the penalty.

But somehow things were different now. Even though Louise was terrified of her father, she pushed her fears aside and gained strength from the promise of freedom. She gained strength from the new resolve she saw in her mother's eyes. While her father was at the hospital Louise did as her mother instructed. She gathered up what they needed without arousing suspicion. But no matter what, Louise did her best to avoid her father. As strange as it may seem, she wasn't sure, if he openly challenged her, whether or not she would be able to control her fear. She was afraid that she would tell him everything, the very thought of which made her shudder.

Three

It was a long drive in the rain, and even with the windscreen wipers on full, it was difficult for Helen to follow the unfamiliar road.

"How long will it take, Mum?" Louise was feeling cramped in the car.

"A few good hours, honey. Have you got enough room there?" Helen asked, aware that her Fiesta was crammed with things.

"Only just. Do we have to take all of this?"

"Louise, we need the sheets and towels as well as our clothes."

"Couldn't we have bought some wherever it is we're going?"

"We've been through this already. I don't know what's in the village. I had other things on my mind the last time I was there." She sighed.

Helen was emotionally exhausted. Running from Mark had meant a constant surge of adrenaline coursing through her body.

Her mind was never completely at rest, in fact; most of her time was spent looking over her shoulder, afraid at any moment he would be there to take them home.

This was the fourth time they had moved in six months. The last place they'd stayed was in Edinburgh. She took a job in a burger bar and found a place for them to live. The bed-sit was too small and wasn't in the most desirable of neighbourhoods, but the woman next door was nice enough to watch Louise while Helen worked. But as always, within a few weeks, fear would creep in, and she would be back to looking over her shoulder, until her nerves were so bad they would have to leave. Louise attended various schools where she was inevitably forced to improvise a new set of lies each day, devising an impromptu history for herself on the spot when answering questions from curious new classmates.

Nothing in their life was constant any more and she hated it. It had to stop somewhere. She couldn't spend the rest of her life running scared every time the phone rang or every time there was a knock at the door. She hoped this time they would be safe, safe enough to settle down and build a new life. This move seemed to be the answer.

It was quite by luck that Helen spotted an advert for a job in a little village up in the Highlands of Scotland. It seemed the perfect place to hide. Helen hoped that she could contain her fears. Louise needed stability in her life, they both needed it. Over and over she thought about the day she came home from the hospital. It wasn't just the guilt and the fear of leaving him, it was more than that.

The day they fled from Mark things had gone easily, too easily, and this worried her. She tried hard to hide her constant fear from Louise; nonetheless, it was always there, niggling away in her thoughts. Mark always said that he knew when she had done something, and deep down she believed him.

Was this all a game to him? Was he playing with her now? Was he following them? She tried to shake these thoughts from her head but they kept coming. She sometimes wondered if he was letting her think she had escaped, waiting for the perfect moment to deny her the freedom she so badly craved. Then she imagined he would exact his revenge, she would pay the penalty, the ultimate punishment – her life, her life with him. She had to suppress these thoughts or they'd never be able to settle anywhere.

When Mark brought her home from hospital, he insisted to the nursing staff that he needed to collect her at 7 a.m. That way he would have plenty of time to make his wife comfortable at home before attending an important business meeting. Luckily, things went just as planned.

Louise rested her head against the door, watching the rain rolling down the window. She would be glad to get out of this car, she would be thankful to stop moving. So many times now they had run. The rain was hypnotic and her thoughts began to drift back to home.

Louise had just finished breakfast, looking at the clock; she began clearing the table. Dad would be home with Mum soon. She heard the car in the driveway. Louise collected her school bag from her room. Hearing her parents' voices in the living room, she stopped briefly to say goodbye to her mum before leaving for school. Louise was finding it hard trying to act as if nothing was out of the ordinary. She was so afraid that she was going to fail her mother. She hid behind the garage, waiting and watching. She felt clammy and hot all at the same time. It was difficult to breathe and she felt dizzy. Her heartbeat echoed in her ears and the harder she tried to pretend that nothing was wrong the stronger the palpitations became. Her father seemed to linger at the house longer than usual and each time she looked at her watch, she feared something had gone wrong.

"Please, Dad, come out," Louise whispered, looking at her watch. "What's taking so long?" Her father always left the house at the same time but today he was late.

"Come on, Dad, please don't stay home." She began fidgeting with her bracelet, knowing that if he stayed at home, it would be too terrible for her mother to bear. All hopes of leaving would disappear.

Just as she was getting ready to run back to the house to make sure everything was okay, her father came out and got in the car. Louise watched it disappear down the road, waiting a few moments before running into the house.

"Mum, Mum … are you okay?"

"Yes, I'm okay." Helen reached out and touched Louise's cheek.

"What took him so long to leave? I thought he had found out."

"I'm not sure, but we should get moving just in case he comes back."

"My clothes are already in the car. What else shall I do?"

"We don't have much time. Go into your father's study and in the top left hand drawer you will find a leather binder. Inside should be our birth certificates. We'll need them."

"Where are you going, Mum?" Louise asked as she noticed her mother heading towards the hall.

"To get some clothes, I won't be long. What was that noise? Louise, it's a car in the driveway!"

Louise rushed to the window, panic blinding her. Helen stood in the hallway, unable to move. Louise could feel the fear taking control of her body. What were they going to do? Louise pressed hard against the glass, straining to see every inch of the driveway.

She sighed with relief. "Mum, there's no one there," she said, her voice trembling as she spoke.

"Are you sure?" Helen moved slowly to the window, expecting him to come through the door at any moment.

Louise reached out and placed her hand gently on Helen's arm to gain her attention before speaking softly, "Yes, Mum, I'm sure."

"Sorry, it's just that I'm so scared. I keep thinking I hear noises." Helen took a deep breath and said, "Okay, let's calm down and focus or we'll never be able to pull this off. You go to the study and I'll get some clothes."

When Helen returned carrying a case, Louise was proudly holding up a bag. Smiling, she said, "I grabbed a few things from the kitchen."

"Good thinking."

There was a strange silence as they stood there, staring at each other, unsure of what to say, each of them trying to gain the courage to make the break and both terrified of the consequences if he walked through the door.

After what seemed like ages, but was in reality only a few seconds, Louise said, "Come on, Mum, let's do it!" Her expression was animated, displaying a bravado she did not really feel.

Helen and Louise packed the rest of their belongings into the car, waited just long enough to feel sure that he wasn't coming back, and then they fled, too scared to look back.

Helen was having difficulty in concentrating, she needed to pull over, she had to stop pushing herself like this. The day they left Mark, she had driven until she could drive no more. She was exhausted. But she was free. Finally free. And yet … why did she not feel free? Where would they go? How on earth would she manage without him? She would have to think for herself, make her own decisions, and suddenly – a world without Mark seemed just as frightening as a world with him.

Helen was looking for a place to pull over when she noticed something in the distance: she could see the lights of the village. She felt a great sense of relief that the end of their long journey was finally drawing near. Helen stopped the car and rummaged around the dashboard looking for the address. She realised how different things looked in the dark and felt disorientated. She couldn't remember the exact directions.

Louise suddenly came to her senses. "Mum, why have we stopped?"

"I'm looking for the directions. They should be here somewhere. Put the light on, please." Louise reached up and switched on the interior light. "Found them," Helen said.

"Okay then, let's go."

"I can't very well read the directions and drive, can I?" she said, pulling a funny face.

"Mum, give that to me. You drive and I'll read," she giggled, taking the piece of paper from Helen.

"Well, stop giggling, and tell me. Do I keep driving straight ahead or what?" Helen smiled at her daughter. It was wonderful to hear the sound of that genuine laughter again.

"Okay, take the next turning."

Helen began driving slowly along the dark road. "Well, that's helpful. Would that be a left or right?"

"Right."

"Are you sure, Louise?" She was tired now and not looking forward to getting lost.

"Yes, Mum, I'm sure.

"Okay, but if we end up sleeping in the car, I get the back seat."

"This is easy. Just keep going until you pass the next bend, then turn left."

"The back seat's still mine," Helen teased.

"Yeh-yeh. Mum, there … quick, turn!"

"Now where?"

"Just keep driving and take the next turning right."

"Are you sure?"

"Yip, just keep driving. When you see Waltz Diner, turn left. That should take us into the start of the village, Mum"

They both let out a laugh of excitement and relief when they rounded the last turn to find Mr Banes, the landlord, waiting at the door of the flat.

"Hello, Mr Banes, I'm Helen Mills," she beamed, holding out her hand, which he chose to ignore.

"About bloody time, lassie, I thought you weren'y coming," he groaned.

"I'm so sorry," she began, but he interrupted her.

"Just hurry up. I'll catch me death oot here," he retorted, pulling the collar of his coat tighter round his neck. It was mid-April, but the night air was cold and damp.

He was eager to be home and out of the rain so there were no pleasantries, no long welcomes, certainly no offer to help them in with their bags; just a quick exchange of keys and a month's rent and he was gone.

Helen got the sleeping bags from the car and Louise carried in a few personal necessities. As they made their way in, Helen switched on the light and they were greeted with a rather dismal sight.

"Mum, this is worse than the last place," Louise said, pulling a wry face.

"Let's not worry too much tonight," Helen said, although she wasn't so sure. She was worried, and the smell of damp in the flat was strong.

"Let's put these things down on the couch and we'll worry about them tomorrow." Helen closed the front door. It had been a long drive.

Although she was glad the flat was partially furnished, it was a far cry from the life they had once known. Mark had exquisite taste. Their home was elegantly furnished and the décor in every room was of soft pastel shades. But she had given all that up, in return for somewhere modest, a place where they could live in peace. Even though the flat wasn't quite what she'd hoped and even though she was exhausted from the drive, she could feel a sense of vitality faintly beginning to colour her cheeks, to warm her heart.

"Mum, it's freezing in here!" Louise complained.

"There's an electric fire, switch it on."

"Do you think it works?" Louise said, standing over the rather battered, rusty looking thing. Louise wondered if it had ever worked.

"Let's hope so, but just in case, would you like a hot chocolate?" Moving was something Helen was getting used to and having something warm to drink was essential.

"Yes please, don't suppose there are any mallows to put on top?" Louise doubted it, but she could wish.

"Sorry love, but I do have a packet of chocolate biscuits!" Helen retrieved them from the bag and was now waving them triumphantly in the air.

"You're the best, Mum!" Louise hugged her.

"I'm glad you think so – and look, it works." Helen smiled as she watched Louise settle down in front of the fire. An overwhelming feeling of affection rushed through her. She knew only too well how much Louise needed to feel settled and secure in her new home. Helen wished fervently that this could be the home she longed to make for them, that they would be able to settle here and, most importantly, to stay.

Helen headed towards the kitchen and it wasn't long before she returned bearing two mugs of hot steaming chocolate. They sat in the living room, relaxing from the journey. Glancing around at their new surroundings, she could see that Mr Banes' priorities weren't his new tenants. She didn't mind old furniture but dirt was different.

With the night-time drinks finished they went into the bedroom. Helen took the sleeping bags and spread them over the bare mattress. Climbing into the sleeping bag, she glanced down at Louise, who was already fast asleep. Gently nudging her over, Helen settled down – tonight there would be no fears, no anxieties. And that was where she and Louise fell asleep. Their first night together in the new flat was, Helen hoped, the first night of a new life free from fear. Free from Mark, for good.

Four

Helen woke the next morning to find a ray of sunlight streaming through the bedroom window. She stretched out her arms and took in a deep breath as a gentle sense of contentment washed over her. Louise was still sleeping peacefully. The room was, indeed, shabby and to someone else may have been terribly depressing. The wallpaper hung off in long strips, black patches covered the walls, and from the look of the wet floor in the corner of the room it rained as much inside as outside. But nothing seemed to matter, all Helen saw were slight imperfections and an opportunity to start from scratch, an opportunity to clean the place from top to bottom – paint the walls, line the shelves, hang curtains. This was going to be their home. When she had called Banes to enquire about the flat he suggested it was in need of a lick of paint, which was an understatement. But nothing was going to stop her from making it a home.

Getting out of bed, she slipped into a pair of jeans and a sweater. A few minutes later Helen was enjoying a cup of tea on the couch. It seemed so peaceful compared to the bed-sit they had shared before, which had been above a pub.

Louise began stretching as she opened her eyes. Swinging her legs out of bed, she shivered, and the sunlight streaming through the window offered little warmth. Grabbing her jumper, she pulled it over her pyjamas.

"Morning," Louise said, trying to stifle a yawn as she padded through to the living room, looking around. The flat looked worse in the daylight. The couch was of brown leather and patched in several places with tape, the coffee table wobbled and was full of stains, and the carpets were damp and smelly. As far as Louise was concerned, this was the pits.

"Morning, love, it's just tea and toast for breakfast, maybe later we can find a shop."

"Mum, this place is filthy!" she grumbled

Helen looked around. The flat might be dirty but she didn't care, waves of excitement and hope washed over her. She grinned at her daughter. Louise's teenage bad temper in the mornings always amused her.

"Well, I suppose it is, but after we've finished with it, it'll be great! Let's get this tea before it goes cold."

They spent the day unpacking and settling in; laughing and talking, they made fun out of the work.

"Mum, what are you going to do with these curtains?" Louise asked, holding them at arms' length from the window.

"I wonder what colour they really are? I suppose we should wash them."

"Won't they fall apart?"

"You could be right, just brush them down for the moment and tie your hair back."

"Why?"

"There might be spiders," Helen said, raising her hands to her face and shaking them as she chased Louise around the room. Louise hated spiders. People passing by must have wondered at the shrieks and screams of laughter that echoed from their humble flat through the street below.

Helen couldn't have been more pleased to see the relaxed, easy expression on Louise's face. They kept peeping out the window as the little village came to life. People were walking their dogs, going to work, and small groups of children were going to school. The villagers who'd lived there all their lives were obviously noticing the new car parked in front of Mr Banes' flat.

"Louise, stop staring out of the window, people will see you," Helen instructed her sharply.

"I can't help it," Louise laughed, "people keep walking around the car and pointing up at the flat." She rubbed her sleeve on the dirty window to get a better look, but the grime was embedded and she finished up with a worse view and a dirty sleeve.

"What do you expect?" Helen chuckled.

"I know, but do they have to be so obvious?" Louise sighed.

"Let's have a look," Helen said as she nudged past Louise. "So they are. We've certainly caused a stir," she giggled.

"No, I don't think it's us. It's that old car you bought," Louise teased.

"It's not *that* bad. It got us here from Edinburgh," she sighed. It certainly wasn't the sleek car she once owned, but obviously Mark knew that car, thus making it a liability. She was certain it would be one of the first ways he would try to track her down, so she'd had to trade luxury for anonymity as quickly as possible.

"Can we go out, Mum?" Louise entreated, looking up expectantly.

Helen nodded, it was time to go exploring and hopefully find a shop or they were going to get hungry. As they stepped out into the new day, the previous night's rain seemed like a distant memory as the sun shone brightly across the sky. Helen took a deep breath as she glanced around. Across the road was a small clearing with a path that disappeared into the woodland. The air smelled wonderful and hearing the twittering of birds made her smile.

Taking a few steps from the flat they turned down what seemed to be the main street. Idly the pair strolled though the narrow streets of the village, where they noticed an odd assortment of houses and cottages. There were a few larger houses, which Helen surmised had been very grand in their time, although they seemed tired in their appearance now. There was also a scattering of farmhouses and cottages around the outskirts of the village, and even though some of the cottages needed a coat of paint and some new windows, it only added to their charm. It was a picturesque village nestled in a valley surrounded by rolling hills and lots of Scots pine.

They soon found a little grocery store. "Morning, miss, you must be the new tenants then in Banes' flat," the man behind the counter said as he smiled at the newcomers.

"Yes, we are," Helen said, surprised how quickly news of their arrival had spread.

"Well what can I get you the day?"

"Can we just look for the moment?" Helen asked.

"Of course you can, lass, just holler if you want me," he said as he began sorting out some newspapers.

"I will do, thanks."

Helen explored the store. She admired the wide selection of goods on sale: there were various tinned meats, cheeses and even frozen ready-made meals. She smiled, it was like a very small supermarket. Soon they were walking back to their flat, carrying bags full of goodies.

Louise spotted the post office. She excitedly encouraged her mum to follow her across the road and into the shop. Helen was surprised at the array of pictures and ornaments and gifts on display. Louise was starting at the local school in the morning and they managed to purchase several items she needed before leaving the shop. As they arrived back at the flat, Helen knew she was going to like living there, and with one last look at the surrounding scenery, she went inside feeling better than she had felt in many years.

Helen had been so busy it was nearly 9 p.m. before they ate. They had a light supper of omelette, served with salad, which they ate in the living room. Louise was sitting cross-legged on the floor, with her plate on her lap. Helen noticed throughout the meal that Louise was quiet; she watched her chase the food around the plate, as if deep in thought.

"Mum, do you think we could stay this time?" she asked, not able to bring herself to look directly at Helen.

"Come over here." Helen patted the cushion beside her, gently wrapping her arms around Louise as she sat down. "I think we could try, would you like that?"

"Yes, I think so. Do you think we'll be safe?" Louise looked worried now.

"Well, he hasn't found us yet."

"Do you really think he'll still be looking for us?"

"Unfortunately, yes I do, but I'm getting too tired to keep running and this is probably the last place in the world he would look." She stroked her daughter's hair.

"It would be nice to stay in one place for a while, Mum."

Helen hugged her daughter tight. She was only beginning to realise just how difficult the last few months of constantly moving had been for Louise.

"Louise, there is one thing: we still have to be careful."

"Mum, please, we've been through this a hundred times."

"Just remember our name is Mills and your father is dead and if anyone asks where we're from tell them Edinburgh, okay?"

"Okay."

Helen knew it was too soon to take their guard down. She knew Mark and he would not give them up easily. The constant fear was a reminder she would never be completely safe.

After Louise went to bed, Helen sat on the couch. Glancing around, she happily admired her handiwork. It certainly wasn't a palace, but now that their belongings were unpacked and they could see out of the newly cleaned windows, the flat showed promise. In a while she would tidy up the dishes and go to bed. They had spent the first day in their new home but for now she would just enjoy the moment.

The next day Helen saw Louise off to school and then began getting ready for work herself. She didn't have to wear a uniform but she was to be smartly dressed, the only other stipulation being that her hair shouldn't hang around her face. Looking at herself in the mirror, she was pleased with the results. The pale blue blouse she had chosen complemented her navy cotton trousers and with the sides of her long hair clasped back, she was ready.

Helen walked briskly towards the hotel, along the main street, just past the grocery shop. She couldn't help but feel a little nervous at the idea of starting a new job. She had never been a waitress before, so it was all a bit daunting. Helen had first come to the hotel just over a week ago for her interview. That was when she met the owners, who seemed a rather odd couple.

The Wilsons were both in their sixties. Mr Wilson had obviously been drinking, but at least his smile was welcoming. His wife on the other hand was a rather stern-faced woman. Helen got the impression that she had arrived in the middle of a disagreement. Mr Wilson suggested that Helen take a seat at the bar and offered her a drink, which Mrs Wilson loudly disagreed with. It appeared as though they couldn't agree on anything, including when she should start work. Helen was listening to the pair arguing, wondering whether she should leave before they noticed, when she became aware of someone next to her.

"Hi, missy, dinn'y take them seriously. They've been like this as long as I've known them."

Helen looked at the man who had taken a seat beside her.

"I'm Banes, by the way, missy."

"Hi, I'm Helen Mills." Helen felt any chance of escaping the Wilsons slowly disappearing.

"Listen, lassie, here's me number, if you're needing a place to stay, give me a shout. I've got a flat to rent."

Taking the note, she stuffed it in her pocket. The Wilsons had finally agreed that she should start work the following week. Driving back to Louise, she had wondered whether to call the Wilsons with an excuse to decline the job. It was much later that she began to realise her opportunity – a job, a flat and a place to hide. She knew she'd take the offer.

Helen looked at her watch. She was going to be ten minutes early, but in her book that was better than late. As she made her way closer, she examined the hotel. She hadn't paid much attention to the outside of the building the last time she was here, but now she could see that it was extremely old, beautiful, but still rather mistreated and shabby-looking on the outside. Even though it wasn't a matter of winning business from the "competition", it being the only hotel in the village, a fresh coat of paint wouldn't have hurt.

She stopped for a moment before going in. She ran a hand over her clothes and checked her hair. She placed a hand on her stomach, to stop it fluttering. Now she was ready. The broken sign which hung above the door read "The Rogue". How appropriate, she thought. As she pushed open the door, the hinge screeched, announcing her arrival.

Five

It was a quiet life. Free time was spent sprucing up the flat, and Helen delighted herself with the fact that everything wasn't perfect. She took simple enjoyment in seeing the scatter cushions, as they sat in an untidy manner on the couch and floor. The village was definitely very beautiful. Helen couldn't resist the long walks in the woods; after all, the countryside was practically on her doorstep and she found great solace in the time she spent outdoors. But mostly she was learning to relax, learning to be free and in the process, learning that it was perfectly acceptable to give herself permission to be happy and to actually participate in life again.

Helen enjoyed her new job. There was something refreshing about clearing tables, serving food and learning to pour a pint – even though it meant long hours and little pay. Of course, there was more to it than that. Mark wouldn't have thought her capable of holding down such a job. Helen definitely felt a sense of pride at the end of each shift, pride in the fact that, *yes,* she could work hard and she could take care of herself and Louise. That was the main drawback of the job, of course, having to leave Louise on her own at night. Even though she was fourteen years old Helen still wasn't happy about leaving her alone in the house while she worked, but for the moment it would have to do, and she knew Louise understood. Helen was aware that her confidence was beginning to grow. She really believed that she just might be able to cope on her own without him.

As time passed, even the Wilsons didn't seem quite so odd. The Rogue wasn't such a bad place to work. It had an open fire which was always lit. There was something about the fire that made the place look homely. Well, at least it was a distraction from the poor décor and the worn furnishings, giving them a sense of familiarity and comfort. There were the regulars, like Banes, who seemed to be permanently holding up the bar, not to mention the fact that if you wanted any gossip, the Rogue was the place to be. The food at the hotel wasn't too bad. Mrs Wilson could cook, even though her menu was mainly hot-pots, Stovies or anything else that could be cooked in one pot.

It felt good to move about the village freely, without the constant urge to look over her shoulder, without fear that she would be discovered. And, even though it was a tight-knit community, the villagers accepted her, for the most part, and were pleasant. There were even a few people who would stop to chat, although she wondered if they were more curious than friendly.

"Hello there, dearie, Miss Mills, is it?"

Helen smiled at the old lady. "Hi, yes. Oh dear, I can't remember your name." Helen blushed with embarrassment. She had spoken to the old lady before, but was absolutely hopeless at remembering names.

"Nan Morrison, I live round the corner."

"Of course, you're the lady with the Yorkshire terrier."

"That's right, dearie. How are you settling in? Will your husband be joining you soon?"

"I'm afraid my husband's dead, Mrs Morrison."

"Silly me, Mary told me that the other day. So you're a single parent. Must be hard for you?" The old lady gently patted Helen on the arm.

"I don't wish to be rude, but I must get going, I have a lot to do." Helen made a quick escape, imagining an entire village of old ladies having tea together and discussing her.

There was talk, of course, as was to be expected – a single woman and her daughter renting a flat in a remote village where they knew no one, had no relatives, no connections – sure, there was bound to be talk. But so far, it had all been relatively benign. Helen was glad when her daughter started school; even though Louise never complained that she was lonely, Helen felt that she needed friends, new people with shared interests who she would be free to spend time with. Louise, on the other hand, was missing her friend Jennie back at home. And at times she was tempted to call her, but so far she had managed to control the urge. She knew her friend would understand – Jennie knew all about Louise's father, but still, Louise didn't want her friend to worry or think she didn't care.

Louise settled into a routine at school and, although she faced the challenge of making a place for herself amongst a group of teenagers who had grown up together, she was doing well. She made good grades and seemed more relaxed, more at ease. Without the constant tension and anxiety that had become such an insidious, destructive aspect of life with Mark, both Helen and Louise were beginning to see a life full of new possibilities.

They had been living in Strathburn for nearly three weeks and life was full of everyday mundane tasks – shopping, cleaning, housework – and Helen loved every second of it. She looked at the clock: if Louise didn't hurry up she would be late for school. Helen was just about to call her, when Louise came into the kitchen.

"Morning, Mum."

"How's school going, love?" Helen asked as she handed Louise a cup of tea.

"Fine."

Helen could hear something in Louise's voice, a flat tone that sent out a clear contradiction to the answer.

"Are you sure? That doesn't sound fine to me."

"Well, sometimes it's difficult, you know, not telling people, and being the new kid makes it worse," she smiled weakly.

"Not telling people what, Louise?"

"For goodness sake, Mum, about us, about Dad."

Helen paused for a moment to study her daughter's face. "Louise, I know it's hard but—"

There was a loud clatter as Louise slammed her cup down on the kitchen table, knocking a plate to the floor.

"Mum, I know! I'm not a silly little girl, remember – I was there." Tears began falling down her face. Helen cradled her daughter, stroking her hair.

"Ssh, I'm sorry. It's difficult for us both, I know. Please forgive me," Helen whispered as she placed a kiss on Louise's cheek. Helen wiped away the tears.

"I'm sorry," Louise sniffed, looking down at the broken plate.

"It's only a plate, love." Louise started to pick up the pieces but Helen said, "Leave the plate, I'll clean it up. You'd better go. Try and have a nice day at school."

Louise placed a kiss on her mum's cheek. "Love you. I'll see you when you get home from work."

"Love you too. Remember your dinner will be in the oven, and come straight home from school."

"I need to run or I'll be late. I'll call you when I get home."

Helen watched her daughter leave, wondering if living in the city would have been better. People there wouldn't think twice about a new face. The city was always full of people coming and going. But then again, that's one of the reasons why she chose such a small village, she thought if Mark came here searching for them he would not just blend in and that was protection in itself.

Sure, things were definitely different living in such a small place, there were obvious drawbacks. The gossip was something to contend with and along with the comfort seclusion provided there was also an aspect of isolation, a sense that she was missing out on the hustle and bustle of the city and the high street shops with their glamour and glitz, where you could buy anything. Now, it was a two-hour drive into town just to get the everyday essentials.

But those moments of frustration and doubt were fleeting. There was only one part of her life that was perpetually empty and it constantly weighed heavily in the pit of her stomach. Since leaving Mark she had cut all other family ties as well and that meant absolutely no contact with her parents. But in all honesty, Mark had turned them against her anyway. And as much as she wanted to call them, she couldn't – they would most certainly tell him where she was. A tiny tear escaped, sliding down her cheek, as the painful memory of losing the confidence of her parents tormented her. The realization had come the same day that Mark's true manipulative nature reared its ugly head.

She remembered that when Mark returned home from work, he was in a rage. She had been out for a drive without letting him know that she would be leaving the house.

"Helen, when are you going to learn?" he was shouting, his normal cool demeanour lost in his anger.

"Mark, please. I just went out for a short drive. I can't stay cooped in the house all day every day."

"You push me to the limit every time! Is that what you want, for me to punish you? Answer me, you bitch!" Helen was too scared to speak. Grabbing a handful of hair, Mark began dragging her across the floor towards the door. The more she tried to struggle the harder he pulled.

"You're hurting me. Please stop, I won't do it again, I promise."

"You took the car out for a fucking drive, you selfish cow. You don't care that I worry!" he screamed, throwing her up against the wall. "Why do you keep torturing me?"

Grabbing her arm, he used his body weight to keep her pinned against the wall. He reached for the handle of the front door and opened it.

"Drive with this!" he sneered as he slammed the door on her arm. The pain shot through her, she heard the bones snap.

Helen slid down the wall. Mark stepped over her and out the door.

Helen sat there on the floor, waiting. "Please don't let him come back," she whispered.

She had no idea how long she waited but somehow she managed to pull herself together enough to call her parents. Sobbing hysterically, she begged them to help her but their arrival brought more pain than she could imagine.

They found her in the living room. Jessie gasped when she saw her daughter. Helen looked pale and her hair was dishevelled.

"Oh my God, Helen! What on earth happened?" she exclaimed, rushing to Helen's side. She noticed that Helen was cradling her arm. "Helen, love, look at your arm. I think it's broken," her mother said, looking extremely agitated. Helen could see the tears beginning to roll down her mum's cheek.

"Mum, please stop crying, it's only my arm," Helen said. The physical pain was bearable: it was the fear of him returning that she couldn't cope with.

"What happened, Helen? Why are you such a state?" Her father looked concerned.

"Dad, I should have been honest with you both from the start, this was Mark's doing. I can't take any more. Dad, I can't live like this."

"Helen, what do you mean Mark's doing?"

"Please Dad, take me home," she sobbed.

"You are home. Tell me, Helen, what you think Mark has done?" He wondered what to do first, call Mark or calm Helen down.

"Look at my arm, Dad, Mark did this to me," Helen said.

There was a dark expression on her father's face. He seemed unmoved by her sobs. "Helen, for a long time you told us yourself that your injuries were accidents."

"Yes Dad, but I lied. I didn't want you to know that Mark caused my injuries."

"What do you mean, Mark? He wouldn't do this to you or anyone, he loves you. Isn't this like before, Helen?"

Helen heard the front door close. Surely now her father would take her home.

"Billy … Jessie … hello. Helen, my God, what have you done?" He was beside her, holding her arm, playing the loving husband.

"Helen thinks you've done this, Mark."

Mark looked at Helen before answering Billy. "This happens all the time, Billy, as I've told you both before."

"Yes, Mark, we understand, thanks for keeping us informed of Helen's condition."

"No, thank *you*, for your support. Now I should get Helen to the hospital," Mark said, playing his part to the hilt.

"Helen, you need to get help. Listen to your husband. Come Jessie, I think Helen's in good hands. Call if you need us, Mark."

Helen's mother was concerned for her daughter and phoned the next day. It soon became apparent from the conversation that Mark had been confiding in her parents. Over the last few years, he had been playing the exasperated husband, saying that every bump and bruise that Helen sustained was of her doing. Mark cried on her mother's shoulder in desperation, concerned that he was unable to keep his wife safe from herself. Helen knew at that moment she was completely on her own. Defeated by Mark and his clever lies, she said nothing in her own defence.

But now, as life was beginning to change in so many ways, she realized how important it was to put the past into perspective. This was a new beginning, a chance to renew her faith in herself, even if that meant pushing her parents from her mind. She began to focus on the positive. Her job. The people around her, the buzz of the village. Strathburn was going to be home.

When Helen walked down the street she marvelled at the familiarity with which everybody greeted one another. She was friendly too, but guardedly so. She had finally found a place where they could live in peace and she was always mindful of not letting anybody get too close. Unfortunately, that meant Jerry, too.

Six

Jerry was sitting in the corner of the lounge bar, staring at his beer, mulling over the day's events, when his thoughts were interrupted by a loud, familiar screeching noise. He'd often thought of bringing some oil to fix that door. As he looked up from his beer, his attention directed to the source of the noise, that was when he saw Helen for the first time.

He was immediately captivated. Her long brown hair tumbled over her shoulders, swaying back and forth as she crossed the room. He imagined his hands sliding along the gentle curve of her waist, her hips. He realized she'd stopped and his eyes moved back to her face just in time to make direct eye contact. She gave him a slow, easy smile. His heart skipped a beat. He ran his fingers through his hair nervously. He thought her smile was warm and sultry, but he sensed an air of vulnerability as well. He watched her. He felt his body responding to this woman and he couldn't help it – he had to laugh at himself. As he shifted in his seat, he laughed at how long it was since he'd felt this way. But it felt good, this feeling – he'd missed it.

Helen noticed him, too. She thought to herself, *stop it, stop it*. She was rattled enough by the prospect of starting a new job, the last thing she needed was to complicate things even more by making eyes at a complete stranger. She had to admit, though, she was definitely intrigued by the tremor of excitement that ran through her body as their eyes met for the first time. Helen made her way to the bar and was greeted by a warm smile from Mr Wilson.

"You're here, lass, and you're early, that's what I like to see. Long may it continue!" Mr Wilson began putting tumblers in the glass washer.

"What do you want me to do?" Helen could feel her legs tremble. She could feel the man in the corner watching her; it wasn't helping.

"Put your things in the store cupboard there and go into the kitchen, the missus will tell you what to do."

Helen put her bag and jacket in the cupboard that Mr Wilson had pointed to behind the bar and went into the kitchen. Mrs Wilson told her where things were kept and made no bones about running a tight ship. Helen emptied the dishwasher and tried to remember where everything went before she was given an apron and an order pad and sent out to the bar to take orders and serve food. Stepping into the bar she glanced around. The man in the corner was still there. She tried to keep busy. She tried to seem uninterested but she couldn't help stealing a glance, every now and then, at his handsome face. Each time she looked he returned a knowing smile. She had to admit, there was a fluttering of excitement that she could not control – and what really scared her was that she wasn't sure that she wanted to control it. Helen had just cleared a table and placed some glasses on the bar when Mr Wilson handed her a menu.

"Take this to table four, Helen, the man wants to eat."

"Table four … ehm," she said, not able to hide a bewildered expression.

"Oh for God's sake, the table near the door."

Helen slowly made her way over to the table. Her legs were shaking, and her heart was all aflutter.

"Hello, your menu sir," she smiled. She thought she was going to melt on the spot when he smiled back.

"Thanks, and the name's Jerry, Jerry Burns," he said, holding out his hand.

"I'm Helen Mills. I'll be back in a few moments when you're ready to order." She took his hand, there was firmness in his touch, but gentleness as well. A shiver of excitement ran over her, her cheeks felt flushed with excitement as she quickly let go of his hand.

"No it's okay, Helen, I know what I want. I'll have the hot-pot and a pint of beer, thanks." Jerry knew what else he wanted. He wanted her. His pulse was racing from her touch.

"I'll bring your pint over and your meal won't be long, sir," Helen said. She could hear the shakiness in her voice as she spoke.

"Please, call me Jerry."

"Okay, I won't be long then, Jerry." Helen's heart was pounding in her ears as she walked away. She had to control the urge to skip to the bar. She was being silly she knew it but it was so good to feel alive and Jerry sparked that feeling.

When her shift finished that night Jerry was nowhere to be seen. Helen felt a quiver of disappointment. Over the next few weeks she found it hard to contain her excitement about going to work and using every opportunity, every excuse possible, to speak with Jerry. Every time their eyes met across the room it was as if there was no one else, only them. Often she would have to remind herself to get on with her work.

Jerry found he was unable to think of anything but Helen. Every night he sat in the Rogue watching, waiting for an opportunity to speak with her. Jerry smiled at himself as he finished yet another hot-pot. He was being ridiculous, ordering food that he could easily make at home, all so he could see her and maybe get the opportunity to talk to her. Helen had been watching, eagerly waiting for a reason to speak with him, and making her way towards his table, she smiled warmly.

"Hello again, did you enjoy your meal?" She could feel her heart skip a beat as he returned her smile.

"Yes it was lovely, but it always is when my favourite waitress serves it."

"I'm the only waitress here, Jerry." She smiled at him, putting her hands on her hips.

"So you are," he said, and they both giggled.

"Would you like anything else?" Her body tingled as she looked into his soft brown eyes. There were small flecks of grey on his black locks, which gave his appearance an elegance that she liked.

"Well, I was thinking about some wine?" He couldn't care less about the wine. It was just another excuse to spend time with Helen.

"Okay, red or white?"

"Well, that depends on you."

"Me, why me?"

"I was hoping that maybe, when you finished here tonight, you would like to help me drink it."

"I see," she said as a tremor of excitement ran through her. What was she thinking? She should say no.

"Well, I'm not sure, Jerry." She wanted to say yes, so why was she tormenting herself?

"Helen, it's only a glass of wine and a chat, I promise. I'll be on my best behaviour." He held his hands up and grinned.

"I would like that, would white be okay?"

"White would be fine, maybe we should get a bottle."

"I'm just about to finish up, see you in a moment."

Jerry watched her walk away. Every inch of his body was trembling with excitement as he thought of the evening ahead. Helen selected a bottle of Chardonnay. Lifting two glasses and her coat, she made her way over to Jerry.

"Hi," she said as she placed the glasses and the bottle on the table. Jerry began pouring the wine as Helen sat down.

"Busy night, then?"

"No not really, just one awkward customer who insisted that I have a drink with him."

Jerry laughed. "I suppose I deserved that after the waitress comment."

"What do you do for a living, Jerry?"

"I'm an architect, rather boring really. So, where are you from?"

"Edinburgh," she sighed. She supposed it would only be natural that he would ask questions. "My husband died in a car accident a few years ago and my daughter Louise and I came here to start a new life."

"I'm sorry, Helen, it must be difficult."

"At times. Could we change the subject? As you can imagine it's a very sensitive subject and I'm trying to put my life back together." At least that bit was true, she thought.

"Well then, have you seen any snow lately?"

Helen laughed, but she was grateful for the change of subject. They talked until closing time. Helen had a skip in her step as she walked home. Jerry offered to walk with her but Helen refused. It was too soon emotionally to move on from Mark. She wished things could be different, that she could be honest with Jerry about her past. What was she thinking? She had no intention of getting involved with anyone. Louise's and her own safety was the most important thing and that depended on their silence.

Nights in the hotel soon became something of a ritual for them, sharing good conversation and a bottle of wine. It became something that Helen looked forward to very much, even though she was a little afraid of the feelings this new relationship stirred in her heart.

It wasn't long before Jerry worked up enough courage to ask Helen out on a proper date. He worried that maybe it was too soon for dinner, but he wanted more than casual conversation in a bar; he wanted the chance to get to know her better.

"Helen, I was wondering, would you like to go out for dinner one evening?"

"Yes, I'd like that."

He couldn't believe his ears. "Great, where would you like to go?"

"You tell me, where's good to eat?"

"We could go into town, there's a new French restaurant that's just opened."

"That sounds nice, but I don't fancy going into town."

He could see she was looking uncomfortable. "Would you prefer Italian or Indian, whatever you would like?" His heart sank, maybe she was looking for an excuse not to go out rather than say no to him.

"Would you mind if we stay here in the village? I really don't want to go into the city."

"There really isn't much choice here. There's Waltz Diner or we could come here to the Rogue if you prefer." He wanted to take her somewhere that was more private.

"Not here. I don't think I could relax. Waltz Diner sounds good." She smiled at him reassuringly.

"Okay, Waltz it is. Thursday at eight?"

"That's fine."

"Okay, I'll pick you up at your place."

"No, I'll meet you there." Helen wasn't sure how Louise would react to her going out on a date. If she took it badly it would only upset her more if Jerry collected her from the flat.

Jerry just hoped that Helen wouldn't be disappointed. Waltz wasn't necessarily what you would call a restaurant, it was more of an up market café, but at least the food was good. Jerry wasn't sure that staying in the village was a good idea. He had suggested that they take the drive into the town, even though it was a good two hours away, because he thought it might give them an opportunity to talk in a more private environment. But she didn't seem interested in the idea at all, in fact she seemed adamant that they avoid the city. So, they settled on Thursday night at Waltz.

Seven

Helen thought that Thursday night would never come. She had only seen Jerry briefly since they made arrangements to go out and even though the hotel was busy, each day seemed to drag. She was worried, at first, about how Louise might respond to her going on a date. Now Thursday was here she felt like an excited schoolgirl as she prepared for her evening.

Helen stepped out of the shower and slipped into her house coat. She was still towel-drying her hair as she walked into the living room. "Are you sure you don't mind me going out, Louise?"

"Why should I mind?"

"Well, this is the first person I've dated since your dad, and I wondered if you would find it difficult?"

Louise thought back to the nights her parents would go out. Her mother always looked so strained and agitated as her father criticised her. "It is a little strange, but this chap seems to make you smile. I don't remember Dad doing that."

"Well, just as long as you're okay with it. And *this chap*'s name is Jerry."

"Mum, go out with Jerry and have some fun. You deserve it."

Helen was deep in thought. True, she was attracted to Jerry and she really liked his personality but could she trust her own judgement that he was really different? She was terrified that his "nice-guy" routine was just an act, as it had been with Mark.

"Maybe I should cancel. It's too soon. I don't think I'm ready."

"Mum, will you stop. Jerry sounds nice, you'll enjoy it. Let's go and see what you'll wear." Before Helen could reply her daughter had gone into the bedroom and happily began pulling outfit after outfit from the closet. "Now, are you going to a posh place?"

"I don't know. I've never been to Waltz." Helen could feel the panic. Louise had a point. What on earth was she going to wear?

"I could always call them," Louise laughed.

"Don't you dare."

Louise ran back into the living room. Picking up the phone, she put on a rather silly posh voice. "Hello, is that Waltz Diner? Could you tell me please, on a scale of one to ten, how posh you are?"

Helen started to laugh. "You little minx, this is not helping me." Grabbing Louise, she began tickling her.

"Mum, stop, I'm sorry," she screamed in between the laughter as Helen chased her daughter into the bedroom.

It was nice to feel so relaxed with each other for a moment. Helen thought back over the unnecessary strain put on their relationship, so many special mother-and-daughter moments that they had missed. She would never make that mistake again. Louise was shouting, disturbing her thoughts. Helen became aware that she was standing in front of her, with her hands on her hips.

"Mum, are you listening to me?"

"Sorry love, what were you saying?"

"I said are you going to wear your hair down or up?"

"Let's decide what I'm going to wear first."

Louise found a lilac dress. She couldn't remember her mother ever wearing it. "What about this?" Louise was beginning to feel just as exited as Helen. She wanted to hold onto this moment forever, life was beginning to feel good.

"Your father hates that dress," Helen said, taking it from Louise.

"Dad's not here." Louise shook her head. She hated how, even now, her father's influence crept into their life, creating an overwhelming sense of guilt. She was very aware that her mother's struggle to break free from her father's control, once and for all, would be a hard journey and it would take a long time for the wounds to heal.

"I know," Helen said, "but he hated this dress." She held the dress against her, looking at her reflection in the mirror. For a moment her thoughts wandered to Mark.

"Mum, stop, forget him," Louise sighed.

"It's hard sometimes, love." Helen wondered if it would ever get easier.

"Try the dress on."

"Okay, why not," Helen said, taking off her housecoat. She slid the dress over her head. Helen looked stunning, Louise always thought that her mum was pretty but there was a glow on her cheeks that she had never noticed before.

"You look gorgeous!"

"Don't you think it's too much?"

"No, it's perfect! You should definitely wear your hair down. Shall we curl it?"

"Why not?" She felt so lucky to have Louise, the only good thing to have come from her marriage. And in spite of everything, Louise was growing into a wonderful teenager.

Louise went in search of the tongs as Helen looked through her makeup. Sitting on the bed, Louise was laughing and making suggestions as to how Helen should wear her hair. There were clothes scattered everywhere and Louise sat with her while Helen put on her makeup, carefully lining her eyes and making sure she hadn't overdone it.

"My hands are shaking so much, Louise, how does my eyeliner look?" It was only dinner but Helen couldn't help being nervous.

"Well …" she paused.

"I knew it, it's too thick," Helen said, instantly feeling what little confidence she had slipping away. Mark's comments were echoing in her mind: *Do you have to smear that stuff on? Can't you learn how to wear your makeup elegantly? Honestly, Helen, you look like a tart, are you deliberately trying to anger me or are you just stupid?*

Sighing, Helen reached for a tissue. She would just have to start again.

"Actually, Mum, I thought the opposite."

Louise smiled as her mum went into a panic over the eye shadow – and what about the blusher, the lips – was her hair too curly? She kept asking these questions over and over again and Louise laughed to try and lessen the pain of Helen's insecurities. Helen was a beautiful woman, she just didn't know it. The one thing that Helen found difficult in her new-found freedom was thinking for herself, and making decisions without wondering whether or not Mark would approve.

She looked at the living room clock. It was only 7 p.m. She had another hour to wait. That was when her nerves really started to get the better of her, when she realized just how long it had been since she'd been out on a real date. She wandered into the bedroom and took another glance at herself in the mirror. Shaking her head, she sighed. Mark always dictated what she should wear and now those familiar feelings of insecurity and self-doubt were back. She rubbed her hands together nervously as her mind shifted into overdrive. Helen used to take pleasure in choosing her clothes for a night out, until Mark began to interfere. She remembered, vividly, one of the nights Mark berated her for supposedly dressing too provocatively.

"Helen, don't you think that dress is too short?" he asked, raising an eyebrow in disgust.

"It's just above my knee," she sighed, thinking that he would also complain if it was too long.

"Take it off, it's too short," he said, taking a step towards her.

"You can only see my knees, nothing above that." She could tell by the look on his face there would be no reasoning with him. Taking a few steps, Mark closed the gap between them: Helen trembled as she felt his warm breath on her face.

"Take it off now or I will," he rasped. Every time they went out, he always put her through the same ritual.

"This is stupid. I've changed three times already."

"Helen, the only thing that's stupid is your inability to understand what I want. Change now. And this time I will select something suitable." He walked over to the wardrobe and began pulling out garment after garment.

As she watched him, a tear slipped down her cheek. She had worn this dress before: in fact he had taken her to buy the bloody thing, so why was he now insisting that it was too short? Resigning herself to the situation, Helen sighed. "Okay, you win." She began taking off the dress. Mark handed her a black chiffon dress which, in Helen's opinion, was shorter than the first.

"This is more appropriate."

After that night she found, increasingly, that he controlled what she wore. Their last few years together, Mark even started the ritual of laying her clothes out for her every day, including her nightwear.

Honestly though, there was something else bothering her. What if Jerry didn't like what she was wearing? What if he was like Mark? Her head was spinning; she was being silly. Jerry wasn't anything like Mark, that was obvious.

She collected her thoughts, calmed herself down and tried to keep the idea in her mind that she was her own person now. She could make decisions for herself. Helen looked in the mirror, and although she managed a smile, she was unsure of the reflection that was staring back. The woman she saw in the mirror looked full of life. She looked happy and that made Helen smile. She was wearing a strappy-topped lilac dress that flared slightly at the knee, teamed with a short black jacket and matching shoes. She pondered over the image before her, feeling there was something missing. Reaching out to the dressing table she selected a plain gold necklace. Pleased with the result she picked up her handbag and went to get one final word of approval from her daughter.

Louise was sprawled on the floor, watching the television, when Helen entered the room. "Well, what do you think, love?" Helen did a quick twirl. Louise smiled as she got up off the floor; she thought her mother looked radiant.

"I think you look great," she said, giving her mother a hug.

"You have the number for Waltz?"

"Mum, stop worrying. I'm nearly fifteen. I can look after myself."

"Yes, I know you can, but I still worry."

"Go and have some fun! I won't wait up," she said, winking at Helen.

"I'm so nervous, Louise."

"Mum, just look at the time – you're going to be late."

Helen didn't get much chance to reply as Louise ushered her out the door and into the warm night air. Helen looked at her watch; she knew she was going to be late. Standing at the bottom of her steps she thought back to what Jerry had said, that the diner was easy to find. She remembered it was at the edge of the village and that was a good ten-minute walk away. She just hoped that she could control her nervousness before she arrived. Hurriedly, she made her way towards the diner.

Funnily enough though, Jerry too felt that each day seemed longer than normal. Busy working on plans for a new development, he had been unable to spend time with Helen over the last few days. Their last encounter had been brief and he had to admit, he missed her.

Jerry strolled into the living room. The shower was refreshing but he needed to steady his nerves. With his towel casually wrapped round his hips, he walked over to the sideboard and poured himself a small whisky. He was soon pacing around his house trying to figure out what to wear, whether he should go casual or a bit more formal. Jerry wanted to make a good impression but he felt out of touch with what to wear. Deep down, he was anxious about going to Waltz for dinner. He wanted their first date to be somewhere more romantic and intimate. Looking in his wardrobe, Jerry felt uneasy. Most of his clothes, he thought, were more for the office than a dinner date. He ran his hand nervously through his hair. He decided on smart-casual.

Jerry took one final look in the mirror: his cream tee-shirt went well with his light tan chinos. Sliding on his light cotton tan jacket, he nodded approvingly. His stomach fluttered with excitement as he left the house and headed to the diner.

Eight

Jerry looked at his watch. He had arrived nearly ten minutes ago. His stomach was tight, his hands felt clammy and his mind began to race. Where was she? Had she changed her mind? Had something happened? What if she didn't come? What then? He could go to her flat to check on her but that could be awkward if she really didn't want to see him. Jerry was just beginning to resign himself to the fact that Helen wasn't coming, when he saw her. He watched her as she walked gracefully towards him. He was captivated by her beauty.

"Jerry, please forgive me. I didn't mean to be late," she stammered. She looked flushed.

He smiled at her, relieved that she was there. "That's okay, though I did think you'd changed your mind," he said, as he shuffled his feet, a little embarrassed by his own insecurities. This was his first date in eleven years, and he felt more then just a passing attraction to Helen. He actually wanted to pursue a relationship.

"I really am so sorry, it won't happen again."

He smiled at the thought that there could be a next time. "At least it's not raining."

Helen felt her cheeks redden at the remark. She couldn't find the words to explain. How could she tell him that insecurities caused by years of abuse from her husband had made her late?

"Shall we go in, Jerry?" She was feeling really nervous now. Even though she had instinctively warmed to Jerry and had enjoyed his company over the last few weeks, she had no confidence in her judgment of men. There was that underlying fear that she couldn't shake.

"Yes, but before we do there is something I should tell you about this place."

"That I'm not dressed appropriately?"

Helen's heart sank. Mark was right, she had no fashion sense. She held her breath as she waited for Jerry to tell her that her dress was not suitable for this evening.

"No, not at all, I think you look wonderful. It's the diner I was referring to, this place is a café during the day and well, what I'm saying is, I hope you're not too disappointed."

"Why would I be disappointed?" she asked with a sigh of relief. But still, her facial expression was quizzical.

"Well, it's not a proper restaurant." Jerry worriedly ran his hands through his hair. He wanted the evening to be perfect and so far his nerves were causing him grief. What would Helen be thinking of him now?

"I'm sure it'll be lovely," she said, smiling reassuringly at him.

"Shall we go in then?" He gestured towards the door.

Helen was delightfully surprised when they entered the diner. The place wasn't very large compared to some of the restaurants she had previously been to. There were about eight tables, most of which were occupied. The lighting was soft, giving the room an intimate glow, and music played gently in the background, making the place warm and very welcoming. The tables were covered in white lace tablecloths and the elegant, long-stemmed crystal wine glasses danced with colour from the candles. The waiter showed them to their table and handed them the menus. Helen was still feeling anxious and immediately began looking through the menu. She had to admit the items on the menu looked very appetising but right now she was trying to focus on something that would help steady her nerves.

"Helen, you look wonderful."

She put down the menu and looked at him. "Thank you, and you look very handsome." She could feel a tinge of heat in her cheeks. She cast a wandering gaze over his face. There was a curl to his hair, giving him a roughened appearance which only enhanced his good looks.

"This place is lovely."

"Well, it's the best we have here. I hope you're not too disappointed?"

"No really, I think it's lovely here." Helen didn't mind where she was, she could only think of Jerry. Their conversation was interrupted by the return of the waiter.

"Sorry to interrupt, but are you ready to order yet?"

"Yes, I think so." Jerry turned his attention to Helen. "Have you decided what you'd like?"

Helen nodded. There was a lot to choose from, it had been a difficult decision. "I think I'll have the steak, well done please, and maybe the duck pâté to start with," she said, looking at Jerry for reassurance.

"Nice choice, I've had the pâté several times and it's very good. I think I'll have the same, only, could I have my steak medium rare please?"

"Certainly sir, and to drink?"

"What do you think about some wine, Helen?"

"Okay, but you can choose." They both laughed. Their nerves were beginning to settle.

"Could you bring us a bottle of Chardonnay as well, please?"

"Certainly sir."

It wasn't long before their waiter returned with the wine.

Jerry lifted his glass and said, "A toast to a lasting friendship."

Helen raised her glass and in return said, "Yes, to a lasting friendship." She hoped it would be long-lasting.

There was a pleasant clink of glasses: their eyes met, and their attention melded into one as they lost themselves in the moment. It was the arrival of the waiter with their starters that reminded them they were not alone.

Their evening went well, the food was simple but delicious, and even though they had both been nervous beforehand, the conversation was light and easy. Helen was relaxed in Jerry's company and she couldn't remember the last time she had laughed so much. Jerry found Helen charming, with a wonderful sense of humour.

As the waiter placed their coffee on the table Helen said, "The meal was delicious, Jerry."

"I'm glad you enjoyed it." He began adding sugar to his cup.

Helen gazed into her coffee, smiling to herself. Tonight had been good but she could not help wondering what it would feel like to be in his arms, to have his lips on hers.

Jerry watched her for a few moments. God she was beautiful. "A penny?" he asked.

"A penny?" She looked puzzled.

"For your thoughts."

She bit her bottom lip, slightly embarrassed by her own thoughts. "I was just thinking that tonight has been nice."

"Yes, it has. Would you like to do it again some time?"

"Maybe we could do this again." There was caution in her voice.

The waiter arrived, to clear the table.

"Perhaps we should go." Jerry stood up, the diner was empty and he was aware that their evening was coming to a close.

"Yes, I suppose we should."

"I'll settle the bill and then I'll take you home, if that's okay?"

"Yes, that would be nice, thank you."

She wasn't ready to end their evening just yet. All the fears she had felt earlier were a distant memory, it would be a long time before she could completely trust anyone again, but she wanted to explore the possibilities, take the first steps to regain her life, and she wanted to begin this process with Jerry.

As he walked Helen back to her flat neither of them wanted the evening to end. She could not remember the last time she had enjoyed herself so much, she just knew it had been a long time. The air was cooler now, but not unpleasant. They walked slowly along the road, the night sky was clear and the full moon shimmered above them. Glancing at Helen, Jerry thought she looked even more beautiful, more desirable in the moonlight. He wanted to kiss her, to run his hands over her. Instead he kept the conversation to her daughter.

"How is your daughter enjoying living here? It must be very quiet for her." Jerry was aware that she was walking so close to him, if only he could reach out and hold her hand: instead he slid his hand safely into his pocket.

"I think she likes it that way, sometimes." Although she wasn't looking for a relationship, she couldn't control the attraction she felt for Jerry. She was consciously trying to walk slowly, trying to hold onto every second of the evening.

"Strange, I thought teenagers hated quiet," he said with a laugh, thinking of the teenagers he knew, with their loud hair and even louder music.

"Well, Louise is a quiet person. I think you'd like her."

"I look forward to meeting her then. I think we're nearly at your flat."

They walked the last few yards in silence. Helen wondered if she should invite him in for coffee, but she couldn't utter the words. She felt embarrassed and unsure of how he would react, maybe he would think she was being too forward.

As they reached the stairs leading to her front door she stopped, turned to face him and said, "Thank you, I had a nice time." She began to fumble in her bag for her keys.

"No, no. Thank *you*."

He had enjoyed himself so much, but now that there was no more distraction, now that they were alone, he found himself as nervous as an awkward teenager and being so close to Helen was not helping him think clearly. He wanted to take her in his arms but he didn't want to frighten her, he thought that would be too much, too quickly. He decided the best thing to do would be to say goodnight casually and suggest that they have dinner again tomorrow.

But then Helen dropped the keys she had been searching for and as Jerry reached out to catch them their hands met – skin against skin. And neither of them wanted to let go. Instead he pulled her close to him, searching her face, looking into her eyes – waiting to see if she wanted him too. She did. She traced the outline of his face with the tips of her fingers and when she came to his lips, she stopped. Helen felt her body respond. She moved closer, holding him tighter and in that moment, just before their lips met, she knew that she was ready. She wasn't afraid, not in that moment.

The awkwardness was gone. He moved his mouth down to meet the softness of her lips, gently at first and then with more depth. Waves of sensual warmth ran through her body. His hand found its way inside her coat and around to her back, caressing her firmly but gently. She closed her eyes, desire running through her body. She wanted more, to feel his touch on her skin. She was arching herself against him. She could feel him hard against her. His hand slid over her breast, just brushing it. She let out a sigh. He went over her breast again, this time lingering there. His warm lips slid down her neck, caressing her with his tongue.

"Stop, not here," she whispered.

Letting her go, he reached down for the keys, abandoned on the step, and looking into her eyes, he could see they were dark with a passion that matched his own. His body was on fire. He had to have this woman. He held up the keys and she nodded. He knew that she wanted him and how she wanted him. They slipped inside and closed the door.

Nine

That had been fifteen months ago, the first night he spent in Helen's arms – the happiest moment of his life – and now it had come to this. Jerry was pacing up and down in the living room of Helen's flat. He no longer knew what he felt towards her. He loved her but it took more than just love to sustain a relationship, there had to be trust and he felt that Helen had never learned to trust him. Whatever caused this mistrust was eating away at the very foundation of their relationship, including any prospects that the future might hold.

Helen was sitting on the couch with her head down. She could not bear to look at him. She had spent the last fifteen months in a relationship based on lies, for which she was responsible. Jerry had given her plenty of opportunities to be honest. No matter how hard she tried she couldn't let go of the past, she couldn't find the strength to be honest.

Everything was such a mess and now her guilt was eating away at her.

"Helen, we really need to deal with things," he said. This was nothing new, he'd said it all before, but this time Jerry needed to make her listen, she needed to understand how he felt. "Helen, you're shutting me out. Look at yourself, you're on edge all the time, jumping every time the telephone rings, even at work you jump when the door opens. Have you noticed the weight you've lost? Do you think that saying nothing is going to make it all disappear? Whatever is wrong, Helen, I will help you; but this way, this silent treatment, it's only driving a wedge between us."

For the first time in more than sixteen years she had discovered real love and now she faced the very real possibility of losing it. He was so different from Mark. When Jerry spoke tender words, they came from the heart. When he offered to help, it was genuine. When they made love, it was full of passion and mutual desire. He was here because he cared. He was angry with her and she knew he had every right to be. She didn't mean to lie but the more time she spent with Jerry the more difficult the prospect of telling the truth became. She imagined herself telling him everything and in her own mind she could hear the words ringing clearly, but fear and frustration kept her quiet. If only she could just block out the past, forget the memories.

For a while she had managed to do just that, living her life in Strathburn, creating her own little world, but now her past was back to haunt her and the pain was greater than before, the stakes were higher. There was a very real possibility that Helen could lose his love. If she lost him life would be unbearable.

Jerry stopped and looked down at her. The last few weeks had been the hardest. Why was she just sitting there? This silence wasn't helping. Loving her was hurting. There were things she wouldn't or couldn't tell him and he was exasperated by the constant way she shut him out. Why wouldn't she talk to him? Something definitely wasn't right and it was interfering with their relationship. Over and over the question went through his mind: what is she hiding?

Jerry knelt down in front of her and, taking her hands, he said, "Helen, I'm here. I'm right here in front of you. I'm not a ghost. I'm not a thief. I'm real. My love is real but you've got to trust me. Whatever it is you're keeping from me, it's destroying whatever hope we have of making a life together. Please don't shut me out like this."

He tried to make eye contact but she wouldn't even look at him. She sat quietly and gave no reply.

"Please, Helen, is my love not enough?"

She was looking at him now. She wanted to reach out, run her fingers through his hair, make everything go away but things had gone too far.

"More than I could wish for," she said with such conviction, that Jerry could feel his anger rising.

"Then why in God's name are you doing this to us?" He heard the harshness in his own words.

"I'm not doing anything to *us*."

This was her last opportunity to tell him the truth. She could feel it but still something held her back, the fear of the past, perhaps scared that he wouldn't believe her.

"Yes, Helen, you are. You won't tell me anything about your past."

"I have, Jerry; you know I was married and that—"

"Stop it, Helen, you know exactly what I mean. You only tell me what I need to know, like the calls, Helen, tell me about the calls."

"I've told you all about them."

"Only that you're getting them but you won't talk to me about them and you refuse to call the police."

"I'm sorry."

"Is that all you can say? Sorry?" He moved away from her, his temper was rising and he was having difficulty controlling it. He knew that getting angry wasn't the answer but by God it was hard not to.

Paranoid was the way Jerry would describe Helen lately. Three weeks ago they had planned an evening at Waltz. Arriving at her flat, Jerry had tried to open the door but it was locked. He thought it odd as he knocked on the door.

"Who's there?" she said, her voice sounding like a scared child.

"Helen, it's me, open up."

The door flew open and Helen threw herself into his arms.

"Thank God you're here," she said as he held her. He could feel every inch of her body trembling.

"Helen, what's wrong, have you had another call?" he asked, leading her through to the living room.

"Yes, but it's more than that. He knew I'd been out, he told me. He's out there, Jerry. He's watching me." She wasn't crying but her voice was nearing hysteria.

"Who is watching you, Helen?"

"Nothing, forget it. I'm not thinking straight. I'll just get my jacket."

Jerry thought it strange, maybe her imagination had run riot with the fright. All through the meal Helen was on edge, so nervous in fact, that they had cut the evening short to go home and only then did Helen relax, slightly. Since then she had become more and more withdrawn, her sparkle had gone and was slowly replaced with some sort of nervous disposition.

She kept insisting that somebody was watching her and she was always on edge. She claimed she was getting threatening phone calls, but it seemed they only happened when no one else was around. Jerry tried to reason with her, it was clear the authorities should be involved, but she would have none of it and *that* he simply couldn't understand. Her unwillingness to seek help from the police and her seemingly unfounded, enigmatic behaviour raised serious questions in his mind. To be honest, he wasn't completely sure that he really believed her. He wanted to help her but he couldn't. As it stood now he was receiving these wild, upsetting phone calls from Helen at all hours of the day and night.

"Jerry, it's Helen, can you come over please?"

"Do you know what time it is?"

"I can't take this any more, I'm so scared."

He knew she was. He could hear it.

"Helen, call the police."

"I can't. I just can't."

Her sobs seemed uncontrollable as she spoke. It was pulling at his heart.

"I'm coming over. Don't answer the phone until I get there, okay?"

"Okay."

Yet again he was torn between his love and the anger he felt. Denying Helen was hard when she was begging him to come over, claiming that she'd received another call, and Jerry could hear the fear in her voice. She was clearly scared. But when he arrived he would try and talk to her, try to find out exactly what was going on, but she would shut him out. The scenario was always the same when he arrived at the flat.

"Helen, do you know who is calling?"

"It's okay now, thanks for coming."

"Helen, don't shut me out like this."

"I'm not shutting you out. How was work? Got any interesting projects lately?"

"I'm not here to talk about my work. I want you to tell me about the phone call."

"I see. Well, I'll put the kettle on then."

She seemed to avoid all confrontations – or perhaps there was something else behind her strange behaviour.

"I can't make it stop if you aren't honest with me."

It infuriated him. When he got there she actually had the nerve to pretend that there was nothing wrong, she spoke as if he'd just dropped around for a coffee. She was driving him nuts.

He stood in front of her now. She wouldn't look at him, wouldn't speak. He knew in that moment that he loved her, yes: but he also knew that he was throwing his heart away pointlessly. He felt he was being used. Whether Helen returned his love or not, he couldn't even be sure of that any more. In fact, he wondered if anything she'd told him was true.

"Helen, I'm sorry. All of this has to stop."

"All of what?"

"All of these lies, Helen. Maybe lie is too strong a word, but you don't exactly tell me the truth."

"I see." She kept looking down at her feet.

"Helen, I need some answers," he said, but there was no reply. "Helen?" Still there was silence. "Helen, for God's sake, don't just sit there, at least have the decency to look at me."

"Don't you believe me?" she whispered, looking up at him.

He didn't have to say a word, she could tell by the look on his face that the answer was no.

"I can't deal with this any more, Helen."

And with that he walked out the door. And that was it, fifteen months of tenderness and real love, leaving. Helen just stared at the closed door. She cradled her face in her hands. The tears were cascading down her cheeks now and she wept until she ached. No matter how hard she tried, she couldn't reconcile the events in her mind, she couldn't find solid footing in her thoughts. Why was life so hard? Couldn't Jerry just be happy being with her?

Was she such a terrible person, that she provoked only anger and disappointment in others around her? Maybe Mark was right, she wasn't capable of anything. The words of Mark and Jerry spun around her head until there was just a feeling of emptiness and profound loss; she was an inadequate human being, Jerry knew that. He had gone without a second glance.

Ten

Jerry stared at the blank computer screen for the best part of an hour; he simply could not concentrate. The more he tried to complete the work in front of him and the more he riffled through the blueprints beside him, the more his concentration dwindled. He sat back in his chair and looked out of the window. There had been a mist earlier in the morning, now the sun was shimmering through the trees. Normally he took great satisfaction from the views of the surrounding countryside but today it gave him no pleasure. Picking up the blueprints he glanced at them briefly before discarding them on the desk.

He wondered what Helen was doing. Did she miss him? She had not called him since the night he walked out. He tried to calm his thoughts. He tried to focus but he knew it was pointless. It was Helen. He missed her and he couldn't think of anything else. He finally gave up and went into the kitchen for a cup of coffee, hoping that would help clear his head.

There were signs of her everywhere. As he passed through the lounge, he reached out his hand and lifted a yellow silk scarf draped over the arm of a chair. Lifting it to his face, he breathed in the smell of her sweet perfume. His life felt so empty without her. He missed everything about her – her laughter, her smile, her touch. His thoughts strayed to the times they made love in front of the fire. Helen had been wearing this very scarf the last time they made love here. He could picture her sitting in front of the fire: she looked so elegant, the meal he prepared was left abandoned as they explored their own desires. He could feel her passion, her kisses. He could feel her soft skin against his mouth. As he imagined running his hands over her slender body, he could feel her hands running freely across his stomach. Jerry's thoughts were disturbed by the awareness of his arousal, those stirrings, that urge to have her. Helen reminded him of feelings he had thought he would never have again.

There had been a time when Jerry's life was very different. It was only a little more than eleven years ago that he was living in the city with Tracy, his girlfriend of five years. They had met during their last year of university. She was studying psychology. By the time they finished their studies, they were living together. Tracy secured a job with the education department and his career was on track. He put in his time with the architectural firm he'd been with since earning his degree and all his hard work was finally paying off. He'd been offered a partnership. He felt that earning a partnership in the firm finally gave him the financial stability he needed to ask Tracy to be his wife. Armed with roses and champagne, he made one final check that the ring was in his pocket before opening the door quietly and listening for just a moment. He wanted to surprise her.

He only took one or two steps toward the lounge before he stopped dead in his tracks. He stood there staring at the scene in front of him. Robin, his best friend, and Tracy were wrapped in an embrace, naked, making love. They didn't even notice he was there. Stunned by the betrayal, Jerry was unable to speak. He turned around and walked out the door. The only sign that he had been there were the flowers and champagne that he abandoned in the hallway. That was the last time he saw either of them.

Jerry walked most of the night, until he finally came to rest on a park bench overlooking the canal. He wept tears of anger and love. Only the night before he'd shared a few beers with Robin at the local hotel. They had been friends since school and had been lucky enough to go to the same university. Robin was a building engineer and they often worked on the same projects. Jerry had always wondered when his friend was going to settle down, get a steady girlfriend instead of the constant flow of beautiful women that he seemed to have. Robin had been telling him of his latest conquest. Jerry understood from the way Robin talked of his new lover that things were more serious, Robin was in love at last. He was happy for his friend. Jerry never would have dreamed it was his Tracy. He couldn't bear to see Tracy after that night and he never returned to the flat again.

To everyone's great surprise he turned down the partnership and moved, instead, to the village of Strathburn. Luckily the firm encouraged him not to break ties completely. He was still able to make a very good living working as a freelance architect. For ten years he got on with his life as best as he could, pushing the memories of the betrayal behind him. He had to admit that he had a somewhat insulated existence, but that was strictly by design. He had no interest in a relationship, he didn't want to experience the pain love brought. Until he met Helen, that is. He smiled to himself at the thought of her. She always laughed at his bad jokes. She was a warm and caring person and he missed that side of her. He knew she had an enormous capacity for love, he saw how much she loved Louise, how close the two of them were. They definitely shared a special bond. He only wished that Helen would let him get that close to her.

Over and over he went through it in his mind. The things that Helen told him about her past were vague. He thought back to one of the many nights they had spent sharing a bottle of wine in the Rogue. "So if you don't mind me asking, Helen, where have you come from?"

"Edinburgh," she said.

"What part of the city? I might know it," he said. He had spent a great deal of time there over the past few years and thought that maybe they could share some memories.

"It's a big city, Jerry. Could we talk about something else; the memories are still raw, since the death of my husband."

Jerry, for the most part, accepted that it was difficult to talk about but, as their relationship grew, he hoped that through time she would be able to talk more freely about things. He hated to admit it, he knew very little about Helen's past; it was if she never existed before coming to Strathburn. Jerry began to put together the fragmented pieces of what he did know about her past.

She grew up in Edinburgh with her parents, but she never spoke of them and as far as he could make out, there was no contact between them and Helen. She endured the death of her husband. Briefly, she mentioned that he died in a car accident but gave no further details. She told him that the city felt empty to her, that she was caught in the hustle and bustle of a place that made her feel like a stranger. She made the move from Edinburgh to the village in search of a simple life. But sometimes she seemed to contradict herself. For instance, her accent was more English than Scottish. And there were other things too, seemingly silly things, but things that stood in stark contrast nonetheless.

One such thing that stood out in Jerry's mind was the time he got tickets for a stage production in the city. Booking a table at Waltz, which they frequently enjoyed, Jerry was excited about surprising her. Leaning over the table and taking her hand he said, "Helen, I've been thinking, since we've been seeing each other for nearly a year, we should celebrate."

"That would be nice, what should we do?"

She knew she was lucky to find love, real love, and had been more than a year without Mark. It was hard to believe. She had a lot to celebrate.

"I know you don't like going into town but I have a surprise."

"Well I don't know, Jerry …"

"Hear me out. I've booked tickets for a stage production and—"

She interrupted him before he could elaborate. "Please don't take this the wrong way but I can't stand plays or musicals, I'm sorry."

Jerry tried to persuade her but to no avail and in the end they did not go. Helen said she hated the theatre. Her explanation had seemed simple at the time. She said plays and musicals bored her and she never really understood what was going on. This surprised Jerry because Helen was an intelligent woman who was always listening to opera on the radio. But then there was an article in a magazine about the stage show *Jesus Christ Superstar*. She had been the one to point it out to him by saying, "You're kidding me, Jerry! You've never seen it?" There was an amused look on her face.

"No, I'm not kidding. Is it any good?"

"Any good? Are you mad? I've seen it so many times," she said, her eyes dancing with excitement.

"Really?"

Jerry raised his eyebrow. He should have challenged her

then: instead amusement crept in, as she excitedly told him all about it and even gave him her silly versions of a few songs. Why had he not been more assertive? Why had he not forced a confession? He knew why. From the first moment he set eyes on her he had sensed her vulnerability: the loss of her husband must have been terrible. He chose patience, hoping that time would heal her wounds, that she would open up to him but, instead, he felt that Helen had totally withdrawn from him. Even Louise, who was a charming girl, never mentioned her past and it was curious that she never mentioned her grandparents. Whenever Jerry raised the topic of their past Louise simply and discreetly disappeared to her room.

Why was life never simple? Why could he not accept Helen for who she was? If he truly loved her shouldn't he be able to accept things as they were? Jerry knew the answer: he had accepted Tracy for who she was, never once doubted her words of love. Jerry wanted more. He needed the security of an honest and open relationship. He needed to trust. He needed to be trusted. The night he discovered Tracy with his best friend he realized that she had never loved him, and no longer played a part in her life. She never tried to call or see him. She never tried to contact Jerry and now his emotions were a mess. He wondered why Helen had not tried to contact him. Maybe she didn't love him as much as he loved her?

Eleven

Wandering into the kitchen, Jerry opened the cupboard door, in search of a filter. This was one of the times he wished he had instant. Scooping the coffee into the filter, his thoughts were still on Helen. Never had his life felt so empty. After discovering his girlfriend and best friend together, he was so consumed with rage, his pain and grief found an outlet through his anger at them both. But this was different. He was frustrated by Helen's secrecy, hurt by the way she shut him out, angry at her lies because she would not trust him and yet, she hadn't done *anything* directly to betray him.

His thoughts were disrupted by a sensation of something falling onto his hand. He looked down to see ground coffee was flowing over the filter. Abandoning his attempt at making coffee, he left everything on the kitchen counter.

Jerry paced back and forth through the kitchen. He simply

couldn't figure out why Helen was so secretive about her past. Over and over now, for the last two weeks, he had asked himself the same questions and still he had no answers. He was hurt that she felt as though she could not trust him, but then again he understood the concept of mistrust. Had he not hidden away in the village and avoided new relationships because of mistrust? So why was he being so hard on Helen? But with Helen it was more than just her lack of trust, she was never what Jerry would have called a relaxed person. She seemed to lack confidence, always trying hard to please him, and at times Helen would get overly worried if she thought she had displeased him. There was something there that ran deep and he was at a loss to help.

Sometimes he found Helen's reactions very defensive, especially when he was probing too deeply.

"What's so important about my past? Why can't you leave it alone?"

"I'm interested in everything about you, is that wrong?"

"Yes, it is. You know that it upsets me to talk about what happened and still you continue to question me. I don't think you care about me or my feelings."

"That's not true, I do care. What's so bad in your past that you can't tell me?" God, she could make him feel guilty. Was he so wrong to ask these questions? She made him doubt his own integrity.

"You don't even consider Louise's feelings – you just say what you think."

He wanted to scream at her, "What about my feelings, don't they count?" But he never did.

Sometimes she would start shouting at him, accusing him of prying into her personal life, or she would accuse him of being insensitive. Her temper seemed most erratic in matters concerning Louise. Although Louise had done surprisingly well making a place for herself in such a tight-knit community, it was also true that some of the kids were giving her a hard time. They were making a big deal about her tendency towards secrecy and they were constantly asking her where her dad was and where she was from. They'd made quite a joke out of her being a mystery girl.

"Helen, it's only natural that others are curious about Louise's background."

"They have no right. They're just picking on her."

"I'm sure it's nothing to worry about." He worried that Helen's need for secrecy was the cause of Louise's problems at school.

"You would say that, you have no idea about children, have you, Jerry?"

"Maybe not, but people, no matter what age, get curious."

"And that gives them the right to make her life miserable? Of course, how stupid of me!"

"I think you're making too much of this, Helen."

"How dare you! Are you saying it's alright to treat my daughter this way?"

And without so much as a second glance, she turned and stormed out of the house. She was so sensitive, and there was anger and hatred in her voice that frightened him. He didn't want to tell her that, perhaps, her own enigmatic behaviour was making it difficult for Louise to fit in.

Then, on top of everything else, there were the phone calls. Surely it wasn't just coincidental that they only happened when he wasn't around? Helen wouldn't give him specifics. She was always evasive, but at the same time she fully expected him to run blindly to her rescue. She did tell him that the calls had started several weeks ago and she led him to believe they were growing more aggressive. At first the calls were silent, then there were strange noises, and finally they escalated to an abusive voice.

One thing in particular that stuck in Jerry's mind was a seemingly offhand statement Helen made. It happened one night after she called him in a panic, terribly upset by one of these phone calls that had supposedly just happened. He rushed to her flat and managed to calm her down. They'd made love that night. Afterwards, as Jerry was holding her, Helen said, almost absent-mindedly, "He's found me."

"Who's found you? Helen, tell me."

"No one, it's nothing," she said as she leaned up to kiss him, but he pulled away.

"Helen, whatever or whoever is frightening you is certainly not *nothing*," he pleaded with her.

He begged her to speak with the authorities but she refused and wouldn't say any more. It was exactly that sort of thing that Jerry couldn't tolerate, being reeled in, put on the spot to respond as her lover and friend – and then being shut out. But he genuinely tried to help: he even stayed with her at the flat for a few nights. But the phone never rang. He remembered one of those nights. Jerry wandered through to the kitchen. Helen was standing over the cooker.

"That smells delicious," he said, kissing her cheek.

"Hope it tastes as good as it smells."

He smiled at her before dipping his finger in the pot.

"Ho, you stop that!" she giggled, shaking her wooden spoon at him.

"Just testing. Tastes good, what is it?" he said, laughing.

"Why you …" She didn't finish the sentence as his mouth took possession of hers. Reluctantly she pulled away from him.

"You're not helping. Lay the table and keep out of mischief."

Jerry set to work. All three were soon enjoying their meal. The atmosphere was relaxed as they talked and laughed. Helen got up from the table.

"Anyone for coffee?" She began filling the kettle.

"Yes, please."

Jerry started to clear the table. Niggling at the back of his mind was the relaxed atmosphere, when only a few days ago the scenario was quite different. Leaning over to lift Louise's plate he spoke to her.

"Have you ever received any of these horrible calls that your mum's getting?"

There was a clatter of cups as Helen spun round. "What the hell do you think you're doing?" she yelled.

"Just asking Louise a simple question," he said, surprised by her reaction.

Helen snapped back at him: "You leave her out of this! Louise, go to your room."

"But Mum …" Her voice was quiet and she made no eye contact with Jerry.

"Louise, do as you're asked, now!"

Louise rose from the table and slipped away.

"Helen, you're being a bit over the top with Louise," he said. He was beginning to realise there was more than just a special bond between mother and daughter and whatever secret they shared, they were equally protective.

"She doesn't need you questioning her."

"Helen, it's been three days now and no calls. What do you expect me to think?"

"He knows you're here. He must be watching me."

"Who's watching you?"

"Forget I said anything, Jerry, it doesn't matter."

"Listen to me Helen, seriously – if you know who's behind all this you've got to tell the police. If not for your sake, what about Louise's? You can't expect me to keep indulging you like this. I can't protect you if I don't know what's going on."

"Is that what you're doing here, Jerry, just indulging me?"

"No, Helen, I'm trying to keep you safe."

"Well, you can't. Nobody can."

And with that, she would say no more about it. Jerry was left feeling frustrated and completely useless.

All too often he found that Helen's mannerisms could change very quickly. He was no doctor, but her personalities were on and off like a light switch – confident, relaxed, scared, agitated, happy, sad, all in a short space of time. Yet the bit that worried him most of all was when she had that vague, disorientated look. She seemed caught in her own thoughts. During those times something about her eyes didn't seem right and she constantly muttered to herself. It was very clear that, when she was like that, she was completely detached from what was going on around her. Jerry noticed it was happening more frequently.

Over the last few weeks Helen stopped going out, except to work. They no longer shared a drink at the end of her shift. Jerry couldn't remember the last time they went out for a meal. She was on edge all the time: she had lost weight and was looking pale. Jerry felt that she was also becoming more paranoid; always looking out of the window and asking if he had seen any strangers outside.

Jerry finally had to consider seriously what had been lurking in the back of his mind this whole time. He had to consider the possibility that all of this was a figment of her imagination. There was the very real possibility that Helen was making this entire scenario up. There was nothing to suggest that anyone wanted to hurt her or was following her but she seemed obsessively convinced otherwise.

There was nothing left to do, really. He couldn't force Helen to tell him what was going on. Deep down he knew that Louise had the answers if only he could convince her to tell him, but he couldn't bring himself to confront Louise either. The only thing he could control was the role he played. The thought of never having Helen again was hard. He missed her. He loved her, for God's sake. But he simply had to remove himself from the situation. What Jerry didn't bargain for was the impact his own feelings would have on him, on his heart. He was profoundly lonely. Helen had given him hope, love, and zest for life – now he felt only emptiness and pain.

Twelve

Helen pulled her coat close. She thought how the chill in the air matched the chill in her heart. Two weeks had passed since Jerry walked out the door and the cold reminded her how empty she felt inside. There had to be a limit to the amount of pain one person could endure and it seemed that she'd had more than her fair share. But Helen had been a victim long enough, and by leaving Mark she'd proven to herself that she possessed the courage and the resolve to make changes in her life. She hoped, most sincerely, that it was not too late to make things right with Jerry. She had to be brave, that was all, and she had to admit that she needed help. That was why she made the appointment, not only for her sake, but for Jerry's too.

Over the past fifteen months Helen's feelings for Jerry had grown. He was a loving and gentle person with a big heart, and she missed his smile, his touch and his sense of humour. Helen could tell that Louise missed him too.

There was always an underlying sense of tension colouring Helen's mood, but, since the phone calls started, she had felt a nervousness growing inside, an all too familiar fear. Her first instinct was to run but she didn't want her daughter to live in constant fear and uncertainty. She decided to stay and deal with Mark once and for all. She didn't want to run. Even though she was afraid, she resolved that she would face the demons from her past.

There was, of course, another aspect to all of this that she must face – Jerry. Over the course of the last year she had tried to tell Jerry the truth, but each time those familiar feelings of insecurity and uncertainty would well up in her chest and she couldn't speak for fear of losing him. It seemed now, though, it was her silence that ultimately drove them apart.

It was only a few yards to the surgery and she wondered, as she walked the last few paces, how long it would take for word to spread around the village that she'd been to see "the shrink". She could hear the rumours now: talk around the village about her being crazy. Trying to keep secrets safe in such a small village had turned out to be a great challenge, especially over the last two weeks since she and Jerry had stopped seeing each other. Work was proving more difficult with each passing day. She kept waiting for Jerry to appear at the Rogue, but he never did. She also had to contend with the awkward questions like: *Where's Jerry tonight? Had a lovers' tiff then?*

The surgery was bright and airy. Helen filled out the appropriate paperwork and found a chair near the window. She was absent-mindedly thumbing through a magazine when she heard her name called. Reluctantly, she made her way down the corridor and knocked on the last door on the left just as the receptionist instructed.

The psychiatrist was in his late fifties, a jolly sort of person with a rather large midriff. He was sitting in a big fireside chair. As Helen entered she looked around the room. Things were scattered around the place and there was an odd assortment of books and knick-knacks. He stood, gave her a reassuring smile and gestured towards a chair.

Helen managed a slight smile in return. She was shaking inside and her stomach felt like it was tied in knots. The panic began to rise and she could feel her heart pounding in her chest.

"Please, take a seat and make yourself comfortable."

"Listen, I'm so terribly sorry, but I think I've made a mistake." Humiliation and fear were taking hold, she wanted to run.

The doctor raised an eyebrow and gave her a quizzical smile. "Well, how about since you're already here, why don't we just sit and talk for a while?" As he spoke, he moved her towards the waiting chair.

Once she settled in her seat he said, "My name is Dr Selby, but you may call me Charlie. And you are?"

"Helen Mills."

Mills had been the first name that came to mind when she enquired about the job at the Rogue. She began fidgeting with the edge of her coat, avoiding eye contact, aware that he now occupied the seat next to her.

Her face was flushed and she felt conspicuous. She didn't know how to begin. She could not speak candidly to Jerry and the only person who shared her secret was Louise. Helen felt that asking her daughter to be her sole confidante in a matter like this was very unfair. Protecting Louise had given Helen the strength to leave Mark, but it had taken her such a long time to build up enough courage to make the final break, she felt a tremendous sense of guilt for putting Louise through all this pain.

"Helen, tell me, why are you here? What is it that I can help you with?"

Charlie looked straight at her. For the first time Helen made eye contact with him. She held his gaze and felt comforted by his expression. She felt it was safe to confide in him, after all she didn't need to tell him everything, just enough to get her life back on track.

"I'm not sure where to begin." She kept her head down, looking at the folds of her skirt.

"The beginning seems like a good enough place. I am assuming something in particular is troubling you, let's start there."

Charlie rested his head back against the chair and closed his eyes. He found this helped his patients to relax and to talk more freely.

She thought for a moment, trying to remember exactly what the truth was and how all of this had begun in the first place.

Friends, that was all they had been at first, but Helen remembered the very day that she had looked at Mark as if she was seeing him for the first time. It seemed very strange the way her feelings for him emerged. She never noticed before how tall and handsome he was, with his blonde hair and green eyes. They went to school together and enjoyed a good friendship and for a long time that was the extent of their relationship. But then things changed. They went from being friends to lovers, then to husband and wife. She even freely admitted that things were good in their relationship at first. Helen thought she was happy, she thought he was happy too. But gradually Mark became more and more possessive of her, more demanding of her attention.

The first real act of violence happened on the night they celebrated their first wedding anniversary with family and friends. He drank too much that night and isolated himself from the rest of the party. She was left to play the hostess: her parents and most of the guests had taken their leave, only Mark's brother and Ian still remained. Glancing across the room towards Mark she smiled. He sat in a corner sneering at her. His face was full of such scorn, his expression so exaggerated, that she honestly assumed that he was joking with her. She wandered over to him and said, "Hi, handsome. What's up? You're supposed to be smiling, remember? I am the love of your life." She gave him a cheesy grin as she threw her arm around his neck. But she was not prepared for what happened next.

"I don't know who you think you are, behaving like this. You're a whore, that's what. You think I don't know? You think all these people that were here aren't laughing at me right now? You both think you're so clever, but I know. Just because you think I'm crap in bed does not give you the right to fuck my brother!"

He raised his hand as he shouted. Everyone stood and stared. He hit her. At first Helen was unsure what happened. Then she felt it, the sting and the heat on her cheek and she tasted the blood on her lip. She picked herself up from the floor, still dazed. She realized through the muffled racket that they were fighting, Mark and his brother.

"How could you fucking do it? She's my wife!" Mark yelled.

Helen ran. She went down the hall and out the door as fast as she could. She ran from the embarrassment, the pain. She walked for hours that night, confused and hurt. She felt too frightened to go back to the house. What Helen didn't know was that this first incident would be mild in comparison to what the rest of her life with Mark would bring.

Exhausted, she finally returned home. She was relieved to find the house empty except for Mark. He walked toward her and gently took her in his arms. "Please forgive me."

She tried to pull away, he tightened his grip.

"You're hurting me," she said, too exhausted to cry.

"I was jealous. I love you so much."

"You hit me, Mark."

"He was drooling over you and I thought you were enjoying the attention. I got so angry and I wasn't in control. Please, Helen, try and understand."

He intermittently begged her forgiveness, in between telling her that she had to understand that he got angry sometimes.

"I love you so much," he said as he smothered her face in little kisses. "But you're simply going to have to accept the fact that I am in no way prepared to allow anybody to come between us and if that means that I have to physically protect what is mine, well, I am perfectly prepared to do that."

But he promised that he never meant to hurt her, although he insinuated that he'd only resorted to such drastic measures because she'd pushed him to it.

When she arrived at work the next day the children at the unit were sad to see Helen with her bruised face and swollen lip. The lies came naturally. She reassured the children that she was okay. They seemed so disturbed that she felt compelled to explain that she'd fallen down in the shower. As the children hugged her to make her feel better, the guilt began welling up inside her.

Guilt, she was full of it, especially concerning Louise. She needed to make things right between them, make up for all those years of pain and bitterness.

Dr Selby watched Helen. She was silent now. He knew the signs, it happened often with his patients. Helen's emotional floodgates had opened briefly and then abruptly closed. Through time he knew that would change and together they would be able to explore her thoughts and emotions more freely.

"Are you okay?" He smiled at her.

"Yes and no. I have to go, sorry." She was confused and felt physically sick. Getting to her feet she headed for the door. He called to her, she vaguely registered that he wanted to see her again in the next few days. Walking down the corridor, she felt stunned; her body was on automatic pilot.

Thirteen

There was a breeze now as she walked the few yards back to the flat. She had gone ahead and made another appointment to see Charlie again, although she was not sure how she felt about it. Even though it made her feel better to share these things with another person, and to hear unbiased feedback, the experience created a wave of complex feelings as well. Talking with Charlie disturbed emotions that she had spent the last fifteen months trying to hide. The fresh air was clearing her head: she began mulling over the events of the last hour. What was it he said?

"Helen, the first thing you must do is get rid of your guilt."

"I can't, Dr Selby, I stayed with Mark. I'm the person responsible for putting Louise through everything."

Deep down what she wanted to tell him was that she felt she was no better to Louise than Mark. She never even smacked Louise but she noticed that it was Louise who was supporting her emotionally. Louise was maturing too quickly instead of enjoying her youth and Helen felt as though she was to blame. She couldn't bring herself to admit that out loud, at least not yet.

"Listen to me, Helen, Mark is controlling, cruel and violent. You did nothing wrong. It was fear – very justified fear – that kept you living with him, a fear that Mark created."

"I don't know if I could face the humiliation all over again."

Her whole life with Mark had been based on humiliation. She thought of his words – *Are you just stupid, do you enjoy people laughing at your stupidity? Can't you even dress yourself with some dignity?* People turned their backs on her when she told them what was happening. She hadn't the strength to face any more disgrace.

"What do you mean by humiliation, Helen?"

She tried to tell him what she was thinking but instead she heard herself say, "Admitting that I was a battered wife. People will point the finger and say there's no smoke without fire. Then there's Louise. The children will make her life hell. They'll blame me and we'll need to move." Things were bubbling up inside, her voice was reaching a hysterical pitch.

"Helen, stop, take a breath, a deep breath, relax … that's it, slow breaths."

She was shaking, scared. What was happening to her? She could barely hear Charlie's words through the pounding in her ears. There was a dizzy sensation and she could feel the panic subside with every breath she took. She was gaining control of the situation.

"I'm sorry. I feel so stupid."

Charlie patted her gently on the shoulder.

"Mark should be the one who is sorry."

Every time Charlie mentioned Mark's name it sent waves of fear rushing through her. There was no *Mark* at home: had there been, she knew the penalty she would have paid for talking to Charlie.

"You're right, sorry, I'm being silly again." She put her head down, embarrassed that she was a grown woman and was acting like a silly child. Maybe Mark was right, she couldn't conduct herself properly in public.

"There is nothing to be sorry for or feel stupid about, fear is a horrible thing to combat. I'll be honest, I can't change what has happened, but if you work with me, you will be able to live with the past."

"Living with the past is one thing but it seems I can't live with the present either."

"In order to live with the present you must learn to live with the past. They go hand in hand at times."

"I suppose you have a point." She was reluctant to admit it.

"Helen, you have to draw a line, make the decision that his abuse must stop. Call the police. Don't worry what they think. You must protect Louise and yourself, then you can deal with the present."

She knew he was right but it was easier said than done. Charlie had been so supportive, not once had he judged her. One important thing she realised was that finally she had someone she could talk to, someone who could help her. There were so many thoughts rushing through her head, Charlie had opened her Pandora's Box of memories and fears. Every strange noise she heard made her jump and by the time she reached her flat, her body felt exhausted, as if it had been put through a wringer.

She felt safe and sound once she made it back home. She dropped the keys on the coffee table and looked around her small living room. She thought how cosy it looked. She admired her handiwork, the bright colours of the throws on the couch and the pictures on the walls, all these things gave her a sense of comfort and accomplishment. She had second-hand furniture and although the place wasn't immaculate, it was a place to live without fear, there was no importance on things being in their right place. She had finally created a home for herself and Louise. From time to time she would find herself lifting a cushion to place it correctly on the couch, knowing how Mark would disprove if she didn't, but it was becoming easier to toss the cushion back on the floor and laugh. It gave her a sense of security, she felt protected from his influence.

She noticed the answering machine was flashing. She hurried towards it, her heart beating faster. She hoped it might be Jerry. As the message played, her eyes filled with tears. "Out again, were you? Miss me?" She knew now that he was watching her. There was no longer any doubt in her mind that he was actually in the village somewhere and she didn't know how much time she had before he made his move. She sat down and for the first time in her life she realized that she must stand and fight back. But even with this sense of resolve, she felt completely alone.

Jerry wanted no more to do with her and, for that, she had only herself to blame. She should have trusted him; she should have given him more credit. He thought her husband had died a couple of years ago in a car accident and she had moved here to start a new life. It seemed like such a simple lie at the time. She was not looking for a relationship, but as time went on, and their romance developed, the lies became more tangled as she tried to hide her past.

There was no choice. Louise would have to go to her parents' house first thing in the morning. Helen might not be able to stop Mark from hurting her, but she would do everything in her power to keep him from ever hurting Louise again. Picking up the phone, her hands trembled as she dialled her parents' number. It had been more than two years since she had spoken to them. Helen wondered why it was taking so long for them to answer, she hoped they weren't out because she wasn't sure she'd have the courage to call back. She was just about to hang up when the phone was picked up.

"Hello." Her mother's voice echoed in her ears, and for a moment Helen thought her own voice was going to fail her.

"Mum, is that you? It's Helen."

"Oh my God, Helen."

She could hear her mother's sobs and it filled her with guilt. "Mum, I'm sorry." She never meant to cause her parents so much pain.

"Sorry? Is that all you can say? We thought you were dead. If it wasn't for Mark, I don't know what we would have done: he believed you were still alive."

"Mum, can we not talk about Mark," she said.

"He's your husband, Helen. Let me tell you the pain you have put that poor man through."

Helen tried to hold her tongue. She tried to remember what Charlie had said: his words spun around inside her mind, over and over again, the idea that she wasn't to blame

"What about the pain he put me through, Mum?"

As always her mother was pushing her aside, rejecting her own daughter for Mark.

"You know that Mark has never hurt you, Helen. You couldn't even call us to say you were alright, do we mean that little to you?"

"Mum, I couldn't call you because Mark would have found me." The tears were slowly sliding down her face. It was too soon to try and make her mother understand; first, she had to understand herself.

"That poor man, Helen, he looked after you, he loves you. How could you do this to him, to us?"

"Mum, let's not go through this, not now. I need your help and Louise needs your help." Stay focused, she told herself softly, remember why you have called.

"I don't know …"

"Please, Mum, for Louise?"

Helen was struggling at this moment. She would agree or admit to anything to ensure Louise's safely.

"I suppose Mark would want us to help Louise. What can I do?"

"Could you look after her please, just for a while?" She prayed that her parents wouldn't hand Louise over to Mark.

"Where are you?"

"I can't tell you. Will you take Louise, Mum?"

"Yes, okay. But, Helen …"

"I know, Mum, I'm really sorry."

The next few moments were spent making arrangements for Louise. The conversation was awkward. Helen felt sadness wash over her. The last few years she had missed her parents but hearing the disappointment in her mother's voice was hard. Even after all this time her mother still took Mark's side. There were no words of love or understanding from her parents and that made Helen angry. How could they do this, take his side? They hadn't even tried to listen to her. But, at least Louise would be safe. The only thing left to do was to face her daughter and it wasn't going to be easy. Helen was totally numb after the call to her mother. She couldn't think about what she was going to tell Louise right now, never mind when she was actually going to break the news. Helen's neck was sore and her head was thumping. She went in search of some painkillers, before heading off to the shower. Now all she had to do was force herself to go to work.

Fourteen

Mark was sitting in his car, looking at properties for rent. A few hours ago he had just purchased a map from the post office in Strathburn when he saw Helen through the window. He held his breath as he watched her across the street, laughing and holding hands with another man. He could feel his stomach churning and it felt as though his heart was being pulled apart. Never had he experienced such pain. How he managed not to run from the shop was a miracle, he wanted to rip this man apart with his bare hands.

He watched until they were out of sight. Leaving the shop, he felt as though he was going to vomit. Taking a few deep breaths he got into his car and headed straight back to the city. He needed time to think, time to control his rage.

Feeling in total control now, Mark lifted his mobile phone. There was a property that had attracted his attention. Scanning the page, he began dialling.

"Hello, Mr Anderson? I understand you have a property to let?"

"Yes, a two-bedroom cottage. Two hundred pounds a week."

"I'll be there in two hours and I want the place for as long as I need it." Mark was used to getting what he wanted and this was going to be no exception.

"Well, I might have other people wanting—"

He cut Anderson off mid-sentence. "I'll meet you at the cottage in two hours. I assume that three months' rent up front will be acceptable?"

"Yes, certainly."

It never took Mark long to size someone up. He was quick to figure out exactly what made a person tick and then it was simply a matter of pushing the right buttons. This was the skill of which he was most proud, a skill that, in his estimation, always gave him the upper hand in negotiations. He had dealt with greedy men like Anderson before: show them a little money and they'd be eating out of your hand in no time.

As he started his car and pulled out of the car park, he thought back over the last two years. That was how long it had taken him to find them. Following his instincts, Mark had begun his search in the cities. He knew Helen well and she wouldn't be able to survive without certain conveniences, luxuries to which she had become accustomed. But she was always one step ahead of him. At first it amused Mark, that is until he lost track of them completely. They were not going to get away so easily this time.

Mark Waters thought of himself as a loving husband and devoted father. He had endured one indiscretion after another with Helen, all in the name of keeping their family together. He had provided a good income and a lovely home and a lifetime of security, sacrificing everything for his family, only to suffer the betrayal of the one person he loved most in the world – Helen.

The morning he brought Helen home from the hospital everything had seemed fine, other than his exhaustion from worrying and sitting up nights with her. But, nonetheless, all that mattered was that she was settled and comfortable back at home. There was something different about Helen, since going into hospital. Mark always considered Helen difficult, but lately she was subdued, answering to his every wish. Although he liked this change, it made him feel uneasy. Mark even delayed leaving the house that day because he sensed something wasn't right.

"Helen, are you sure you'll be fine?"

"Yes, I'm sure. But if you think I won't cope, it would be nice to have you home," she said, smiling ever so sweetly.

"Promise me you won't move from the couch. You've got the phone right here. You call *me* if you need anything."

"I promise, stop fussing. You are wonderful Mark, thank you."

He went to work, business as usual, but he couldn't shake that niggling feeling inside. He couldn't concentrate. He didn't make it halfway through the morning before he became obsessed with thoughts of Helen.

He was concerned for her, that's what he told himself, and when she didn't answer the phone after repeated attempts, he went home to check on her. Opening the front door, he called out for her, "Helen, Helen where are you?" His voice echoed through the house. "Helen, answer me now!" Panic rushed over him as he raced from room to room.

It didn't take long to realize that she'd abandoned him and taken Louise too. He called her parents, they said they knew nothing and he believed them. He kept telling himself she would be back soon; she didn't have the guts or the gumption to leave him. But as the new morning dawned, Mark knew she wasn't coming back.

In a fit of rage he gathered her belongings. He searched out her special boxes of *"memories"* as she called them: Louise's first shoes, birthday cards, handmade Mother's Day cards, they were full of what he would call rubbish. He collected anything on which Helen placed any sentimental value and he burned every bit of it – everything reduced to ashes before his eyes.

Taking indefinite leave from work, he began his search. He would make her pay the penalty for her deceit and disloyalty. Mark traced her car to a garage in Edinburgh. The mechanic gave Mark her address, but he was too late, she was no longer there. He smiled. She thought she was so clever, moving from place to place, except for one small mistake. In the last hovel she stayed in, Helen had made friends with a young lady next door and even asked her to check on Louise while she made an overnight trip to a village somewhere in the Highlands for a job interview. Once he was armed with this information, Mark simply travelled in a logical fashion, arriving at each village and staying long enough to determine if his loving wife was there.

He had to admit, Helen was intriguing him. She braved the elements of living beneath the standards that he provided her. He finally found her living in a ratty flat, in the tiny village of Strathburn.

A heavy-set man was lurking in the doorway of the cottage. Anderson had been there for the last ten minutes, waiting. He'd been so pissed-off with the call regarding his cottage that he was prepared to give this man, if he ever got there, a piece of his mind. But the longer Anderson stood there, the more his greed took over. He could do a lot with two and a half thousand quid. His thoughts were disturbed by the sound of an approaching vehicle. Mark pulled his Rover into the driveway.

"Hi there mate, Anderson's the name," he said, holding out a hand which Mark ignored.

"You'll want your rent," Mark said. As far as Mark was concerned Anderson was a greedy slime ball.

"The rent, yes, up-front as agreed. And what's your name then, for records, of course?" Anderson asked. He could smell the money from this man with his fancy car and was very interested in his new tenant.

"Mark Waters is the name, charming place you have here." Mark doubted there would be any such records, but if he expressed curiosity he knew it would ruin everything.

"She's charming alright, did the work myself," Anderson said, beaming with pride.

Charming was not the word Mark wanted to use. The cottage was as run down as the rest of the village. The sooner he could get rid of Anderson the quicker he could deal with his beloved Helen.

Mark opened the door to his new residence and went in, followed by Anderson. It was not what he was used to but it would do. The décor hadn't been touched in years. The wallpaper was faded and the white paint had a yellow tinge. Mark sat down on the lumpy couch. He was convinced it was stuffed with horse hair, at least it smelled like horse hair. The rest of the cottage was sparsely furnished. Mark ran his finger through the white dust on the mantelpiece. He hated dirt.

He only saw the discomfort as a means to an end, something else he would have to tolerate because of Helen. He was mentally prepared to do whatever was necessary. Mark thought other things through as well. He had bought plenty of provisions in the city. People in little villages talk and he wasn't going to be too obvious, at least not yet. Anderson was a fool. Mark told him that he was trying to complete his first novel so had exchanged the distractions of city life for the peace and quiet of a small village, a story Mark knew Anderson would find completely uninteresting and thus not worth repeating.

With very little prompting, Anderson was all too eager to tell Mark about the new girl in the village. "A nice looking filly. Lucky sod, that Jerry Burns, putting her through her paces, if you get what I mean." Mark wanted to kill Anderson then and there but, as annoying as he might be, he would be a useful source of information.

As Mark unpacked his supplies he thought of Helen. He thought of how she'd pleaded and begged him all these years to believe that she was faithful, trustworthy. He could hear her now, repeating those familiar words. *Please, Mark, don't say these things. I love you. Mark, I swear I have never been with another man since the day I met you.* He thought of how she cried. But for all her begging and pleading it turned out he had been right about her character all along.

The first chance she got she showed him her true colours and proved him right by abandoning their life together and falling quickly into another man's bed. He thought of their wedding day, their vows – till death do us part. He intended to be faithful to those vows and he was going to make sure Helen was too.

Mark spent the next few days carefully gathering information. He knew where Helen lived. He watched Louise go to school, standing so near that he could have reached out and touched his daughter. But he had to control himself, at least for a while. The difficult part was watching his beloved Helen in the arms of another man. It was like a scene from his worst nightmare playing out before his eyes. Mark was clenching his fists. He had actually seen them kissing, Helen allowing him to run his hands over her body and not caring that anyone saw her. She openly wanted him, like a bitch on heat. Sometimes it was all he could do to restrain himself, to keep from destroying them both. But as usual, he thought, he was the one to sacrifice himself, to hold those impulses in check. He sacrificed his own desires to bring their family back together.

Fifteen

Anderson's cottage might be old and rather neglected but it was in an ideal position, just on the outskirts of the village. Mark soon discovered that a short walk through the woods brought him to a small clearing from which he had a good view of Helen's flat. He could watch her every move from that vantage point.

He became well acquainted with all aspects of Helen's life, no detail was too small. He kept meticulous notes of all her comings and goings and it wasn't too long before he felt confident enough to put his plan into action. Mark dialled her number.

"Hello? … Hello, hello is anyone there?"

He couldn't speak, her sweet tone echoed in his ear and he smiled as the line went dead. Mark had forgotten how sweet Helen's voice sounded. He had been so happy when Helen agreed to marry him and for a while the marriage had been good. He helped her, guided her, he thought. He gave Helen everything she wanted but, of course, it wasn't enough. She sought attention from other men.

Where had he gone wrong? He certainly wasn't like his father. His father allowed his mother to work, to have her own independence, friends. The house was never tidy and she was never home. And for a long time Mark thought his mother's absence was because she resented him, that he was restricting her freedom. When he found his mother in the arms of another man, he never spoke to her again. Mark's father never got over losing her. Mark blamed his father, though. His mother's behaviour was a direct consequence of his father's neglect, allowing her to do as she wished, never setting rules and having no expectations. As soon as Mark was able, he left home and never returned. When he married Helen he stipulated certain things – a tidy home, giving up her job, a woman's place is in the home. But he was by no means selfish, he was more than happy to take her wherever she needed to go.

Sadly enough, although he never actually found her with other men, he simply knew. It became unbearable when he felt her repulsion to his touch. In these moments he felt close to madness, she drove him to the brink of all reason, but he had to protect his own. So, he began the ritual of calling when she was on her own to remind her, "You will always belong to me, Helen, you can't escape me."

Right now though, as Mark watched Helen's flat from the clearing, the hardest part was knowing that Jerry Burns was there with her. For three days he had not left Helen's side. Mark was consumed with jealousy. Had he not given her everything she could possibly want and more, yet she expected him to put up with these indiscretions?

Helen was now on her own, Burns had finally gone. So consumed with rage, the only thing left to Mark was to vent his anger and frustration in his calls: they became more and more abusive.

Standing at the edge of the woods watching Helen certainly gave Mark plenty of time to think, and he knew one thing for sure – he never wanted to smell Scots pine again. That wretched, overbearing odour seemed to cling to his clothes long after he left the woods. He had stepped up surveillance over the last few weeks and noted that Burns no longer came around. At first Mark thought that he was away on business, but he found out this was not the case. Anderson took great delight in telling him that Helen was a free agent.

"If you ever get lonely out here, you should come down to the Rogue, have a pint."

"Well maybe, but I must concentrate on this novel." Mark managed a weak smile, this man made him feel sick, but he played along, at least for the moment.

"What's this book about then?" Anderson asked, hoping it was something raunchy.

"It's a very interesting subject, based on the policies of taxation in the late seventeen century."

Anderson stood staring. He only read the occasional under-the-counter magazine or rather, just looked at the pictures. Thinking Mark was ready to explain more about his book he changed the subject. "Talking about the Rogue, that bit of stuff, you know the one, the new lass. Seems Burns lost interest in her, silly bastard."

"I see, fancy your chances then?" Mark grimaced. Surely even Helen wouldn't stoop that low.

"Have to say, wouldn't mind taking her home on a cold night, eh? Think it's about time for a pint."

As Mark remembered Anderson's words, he fixed his thoughts on the idea of Helen being on her own again. Mark smiled. He hoped that Helen would realize now that not many men would put up with her bad behaviour, not as he had done all these years.

There was movement at Helen's flat, something caught his attention, bringing him back to his immediate surroundings, focusing his attention on the task at hand. Helen appeared at the door and was putting some bags in the car. Within a matter of moments both Helen and Louise were in the car and pulling away. That's ok, he thought – it wouldn't be difficult to find out where they were going. Mark had other things on his mind, Jerry Burns in particular. Making his way back to the cottage, Mark retrieved a long box from the car, a little something which he had put together a few days ago, for that special moment. "A little gift for you, my love," he whispered.

Leaving the package at Helen's door he decided it was time to pay Jerry Burns a visit.

Weaver's Cottage – that was what it was called. A hundred years old, that was what it was, but that didn't interest Mark. He wasn't here for a history lesson: it was the present that interested him. As he walked up the path to the front door, he admired the cottage's renovation. This man has taste, he thought. He had collected as much information on Burns as possible beforehand and he knew that he was an architect, a good one at that, and with Anderson's help he had traced Burns' background. He knew all about his last relationship. Surely he would understand the torture of being betrayed by love. He took a deep breath and knocked loudly on the door.

"Hello, Mr Burns. I'm Mark Waters. I think we should talk." He held out his hand as a gesture of greeting, but Jerry just stared. For some reason he felt an instant dislike for this man.

"I see. Well, better come in then." Jerry showed Mark into the living room and gestured him towards a seat. It felt strange having this man in his house. He could feel every hair prickling at the back of his neck.

"Well?" Jerry raised an eyebrow as he spoke.

"I want to discuss Helen with you. You see, I am her husband." He smiled, watching Jerry's face, enjoying the pained look in his eyes.

Jerry tried to stay calm. "I see …" Almost like a reflex, images of Tracy's betrayal flashed before him.

"Let me guess. She told you I was dead? Now, let's see … what was it this time? Did I commit suicide or was it a car crash?" Mark smiled. When Anderson first told him Helen was a widow he was full of rage but now, it was a different feeling. The look on Jerry's face said it all. Mark knew that he had Jerry's full attention and with that he began to discuss his wife.

"Helen was a fragile girl, always falling, having accidents. At least, that's what she told me. But after the birth of our daughter I began to realise that things were more serious. She lied to me. They weren't accidents. She had done these things to herself."

"What do you mean, accidents?" Jerry didn't think of Helen as fragile in that way. He had never known her to have an accident.

"Increasingly, I would come home from work and find her covered in cuts and bruises. Thankfully, she never harmed Louise. In the end I tried everything, even coming home from work during the day to make sure she was safe. Then she started to leave the house and wander, unsure of whom she was. I tried to gently suggest that she should call me when she needed to go out and I would come home and take her, but she refused." Mark paused, surmising that Jerry couldn't cope with deceit or he wouldn't be hiding in this little village. He decided to play on guilt and pity and manipulate this man's sorrow, use it to his advantage.

Jerry's immediate response was to assume this man was talking about someone else, surely he was. "I've never seen Helen with cuts and bruises and she has no problems getting around the village."

"If you'll let me go on, I'm sure you'll begin to understand." Mark realised this was going to be harder than anticipated, this man was not stupid. He would have to reel him in slowly.

"Be my guest," Jerry said, his voice full of sarcasm.

"Dr Brewster, a well respected man in his field, treated Helen with drugs. They helped for a while but then she would stop taking them and it was during these times that she would run away from home. This is one of those times, Jerry, and it has been the longest so far. It was hard to find them this time, but thankfully Louise called me. She'd been trying for months and months, but I'd been on the road, looking, searching, and feeling that this time I had lost them. Then, returning home, I found a frantic message from Louise asking for me to come and get her. Now I have to think about the next step. I've contacted Dr Brewster. He'll be here in a week or so. I hope he can persuade Helen to return to his clinic for treatment, before coming home – if she comes home."

Jerry found this difficult to listen to; none of it made sense. He couldn't sit here and listen to this. He refused to believe any more of these stories, these accusations. Could this be what Helen was hiding? It seemed too simple. "Listen, Mr Waters, I think it would be better if you left," Jerry said.

"Listen, Jerry, may I call you Jerry? My wife is ill. I need your help." Mark could see glimmers of pain, at times anger, on Jerry's face and this pleased him. Now Jerry would have a taste of pain the likes of which Mark had been forced to endure since Helen deserted their marriage.

"I don't think that's possible," Jerry said, his gut feeling telling him that there was no way he was going to help this man.

"Don't you care about her, Jerry?"

"Yes I do, but ..."

"Then help me, maybe we should have a drink to ease the situation?" Jerry didn't like the idea one bit, he wanted Mark to leave. But what if he was telling the truth? He would have to hear him out.

"Whisky okay?"

Mark nodded. He felt so close, the only thing standing in the way of Helen coming home was Jerry, and that was about to change.

Sixteen

Jerry handed Mark a glass. He began pacing back and forth. Jerry's mind was in turmoil. He took a deep drink of whisky. He could feel the heat as it slid down his throat. There was so much he wanted to ask, but was afraid of the answers.

"Is *Mills* Helen's maiden name?" he asked, searching for an honest thread, something that Helen was truthful about.

"No, it's Baker."

"And Louise was the one who called you?"

"Thankfully yes," Mark said, looking into his glass, watching the whisky dance as he swirled the ice. It was all a game of patience now, he was aware that he would have to give Jerry the opportunity to ask questions.

"So why didn't Louise tell me any of this?"

"Things are difficult for my daughter, never mind the embarrassment of telling you about her mother."

It amazed Jerry how relaxed Mark seemed about the whole situation.

"Please, don't look so shocked. Helen's condition has become worse over the years. At times she lives in a completely different world with different identities. With each new identity she starts moving around all over the place, renting flats and telling terrible lies about how badly she's been mistreated. It's been awful. I love my wife but I'm getting to the point where I can no longer live this way and I must seriously consider having her committed for her own safety, depending on what the doctor recommends."

"What kind of doctor is this Brewster?"

"He is a psychiatrist and extremely good with Helen," Mark said, trying not to smile. Jerry already seemed full of doubts about Helen, all he had to do was tease them out, work them to his advantage.

"I see. You want him to commit Helen then. On what grounds?"

"Helen is mentally unstable." He noted the brief but definite change in Jerry's facial expression.

"I only have your word for that," he sneered, trying to control his anger.

"I realise that, but I would not be seeking you out unless it was true."

"Yet again, I only have your word for that too." There was an eerie silence as Mark allowed Jerry a few moments to contemplate the situation before continuing.

"Every time she runs away and I go searching for her, I find she's told everyone that I'm dead. This is very sad since I am the only person Helen has to look after her. She caused so many scenes with her parents, telling them that I beat her that now, they no longer speak to her. It's terribly sad."

"Are you telling me that Helen does this all the time?"

"Sadly, yes, and you are not the first."

Jerry flinched as the remark hit home. "This is Helen you're talking about, you can't expect me to believe this story." Even though Jerry wanted to stand by that statement, Mark had actually given a plausible explanation and even though his heart was breaking, things were beginning to slot together.

"You must realize that your relationship with Helen is based on fantasy."

"What fantasy?" Jerry asked.

"The world she creates inside her own head. What you need to understand, Jerry, is that when she starts her medication you will be nothing more than a fuzzy memory. I'm sorry, but I've had to do this so many times."

The more this man talked, the less Jerry liked him. He should be feeling pity for him, instead there was only hatred.

"I love her, Mark, and you're making her out to be some sort of monster." He couldn't consider this man's feelings now, he couldn't help being in love with Helen.

"No, I'm not. But Jerry, she is ill. All this is difficult, I do understand. There's nothing worse than finding out the person you care for the most, doesn't love you as much as you thought."

Jerry searched Mark's face. He was saying the words, but there was no emotion. He was sure that every now and then his eyes held a glint of amusement.

"This can't be happening." Jerry sat down in the chair, leaning forward to cradle his head in his hands. He doubted his own judgment and all his thoughts were spinning wildly inside his head, set in a flurry of motion by the possibility that this man could be telling the truth.

"What can I say to make you believe me? Has she been pestering you, calling at all hours of the night, asking you to come around saying that someone is calling her and watching her every move?"

"Yes she has, but …" He paused, he was looking for another reason why she was calling but he couldn't come up with a plausible explanation.

"So, she has been calling. Did she tell you that I was dead?" Mark asked, raising an eyebrow in a quizzical fashion.

"Yes," Jerry said, his voice was hardly audible.

"Think, Jerry, how many times has she been irrational, difficult to handle?"

"What do you mean, difficult to handle? You don't *handle* people." Jerry was seething, gritting his teeth.

"What about Louise? Haven't you noticed how protective she is of her mother, you must have noticed that?" he smiled.

Jerry had noticed. He knew their relationship was more than a close bond. This man was only saying what he already thought, but he could feel the anger rising within him anyway. He wanted to smack this guy in the jaw. This was Helen he was discussing, but not the woman Jerry had come to love. He was making her out to be a freak. But Jerry refrained. After all, what he said, sadly enough, was making sense. Jerry had suspicions himself that everything was all in her head, but he had to be sure. He did not know this man but he definitely seemed to know Helen. His thoughts were interrupted by the phone ringing. He picked it up.

"Hello."

"Jerry? It's Helen. Please, listen to me. Please. I'm sorry about everything. I'm sorry, please, can you come over?"

There was something in her voice. How could he tell her there was a man here who said he was her husband?

"I don't think that's a good idea." His reply was sharp. He knew it.

"Please. Something has happened." She was sobbing now.

"What's happened?"

"I can't tell you over the phone. Please, I have no one else to turn to, Jerry."

He was conscious of not using Helen's name, aware that Mark was listening intently.

"I'll be there in a minute." It all sounded like more of the same vicious cycle to him – the begging and pleading and urging him to run to the rescue, only to find her acting evasively, as if nothing was actually wrong. But he had to see Helen. Selfish as it sounded, he had a reason to go and see her but he also wanted answers. He needed to know the truth.

"Excuse me please, I have to go out." He gestured towards the front door. Mark stood up.

"Please, I ask of you, say nothing. If she runs with Louise again, I may not find them this time." He shook hands with Jerry and started to leave. He turned around and said, "Jerry, ask Helen to tell you what she did to the cat."

Mark walked away, grinning to himself. It was obvious that Helen was the caller; Burns was awkward when he answered the phone. She must have received his flowers: all he could do was sit back and wait. He was relying on Helen now, her inability to behave, to be honest. If she could lie to him then she would lie to Burns. Mark had only given his doubts a helping hand.

Jerry walked to Helen's house, thinking about what Mark had said. It was unfair to condemn Helen without a fair hearing. Jerry felt confused and the only thing he knew for sure was that life was beginning to feel like hell. He no longer knew what he believed. Deep down, he wanted Helen, but the more Jerry mulled the events over in his mind the more Mark made some sort of weird sense. He had known for some time that Helen and Louise were hiding their past. Louise seemed happy living in the village, but if Mark was right and Louise was simply biding her time, waiting for an opportunity to call Mark, then Jerry had serious reason to doubt his own judgement.

Seventeen

Last night had been the first time Helen had spoken to her parents since leaving Mark. She was glad they had agreed to take Louise for a while. Helen didn't know how Mark had found them but she had absolutely no intention of subjecting Louise to any more unnecessary drama. How was she going to make Louise understand that she would have to go away? A doubt began creeping in, was she doing the right thing sending her daughter away? Maybe this was Mark's intention. Maybe he was trying to separate them. If he got hold of Louise then he would force Helen to return home. Helen looked at the clock. Louise would be leaving for school soon, there would be no time to talk now, and maybe it was just as well, she was scheduled to see Charlie Selby this morning. It gave her an excuse to avoid speaking to Louise about the approaching visit to her grandparents, assuring herself that she didn't have the strength to face both of them in such a short time.

"Come on, Louise, hurry or you'll be late for school," Helen shouted down the hallway.

"I'm coming, Mum," Louise called as she rushed into the living room. "I don't have time for breakfast this morning. Are you okay?" Louise had never see her mother quite so pale.

"Yes, love, I just have a lot on my mind."

"We're not moving again are we?" Louise said, sighing. That fear was always in the back of her mind, that she would spend her life drifting from place to place.

"No, no, nothing like that. It's just work," she said as guilt flowed over her. It was actually Louise who was moving.

"Are you sure? You've been acting a bit strange lately." Louise couldn't help but notice that her mother jumped at the slightest noise and just yesterday she had yelled at Louise, accusing her of sneaking up on her.

"Well, I suppose I have, what with the situation with Jerry and stress at work, but honestly, I'm okay." Helen shifted her feet – lying to Louise filled her with guilt.

"I have to go," Louise said. The truth was that she missed Jerry too. She thought he was fun and until lately had made her mum very happy. Mum wouldn't tell her why she and Jerry had stopped seeing each other but whatever had happened it was making her ill.

"Enjoy school," Helen said, trying to smile for Louise's sake.

"See you later, Mum." She kissed Helen on the cheek.

"Have a nice day, my love." The door closed, Helen sighed. She couldn't put off telling Louise indefinitely, but how was she going to tell her? Helen didn't know.

Helen walked down the street, towards the surgery. Doctor Selby had insisted that they should meet today. He held two sessions a week at the surgery and felt that Helen, for a short time, would benefit from seeing him twice a week. Helen wasn't so sure her emotions had recovered from their last meeting, everything still felt raw inside.

As she entered the surgery the receptionist smiled at her and said, "Good morning, Miss Mills, are you seeing Dr Selby again?" The nurse nodded knowingly.

"Yes, thank you." Helen glanced around the waiting room; at least it was relatively empty. Her cheeks were hot with embarrassment as she sat down and buried her head in the first magazine she could find. She didn't have long to wait.

"Dr Selby will see you now, Miss Mills," called the receptionist.

"Thank you," Helen said, swiftly making her way down the corridor. Charlie was waiting at the door of his room.

"Good morning," he said, greeting her with a smile as he held out his hand. Helen smiled back warmly as she shook it. They made their way into the room, and he gestured for her to take a seat.

"How have you been since we last spoke, Helen?"

"Well, actually, I have been on edge lately."

"I see, well, that will happen as we explore your emotions and as we deal with them. You should feel stronger, more in control of your own life, as we progress." He smiled in an understanding way.

"I suppose that's what I want, to be in control of my life and to be my own person, but every time I turn a new corner it gets harder." She was thinking now of the whole mess with Jerry. Everything had changed so quickly and she had no control over anything.

"Helen, we spoke about the first time Mark was violent towards you. Do you know when things changed, when love was taken over by fear?"

Helen thought for a moment, and then as she remembered, a cold chill ran through her. She would never forget the night she realized that Mark had no boundaries in his obsessions.

"Yes, unfortunately I do," she said, taking a deep breath.

Charlie nodded to her, gesturing for her to continue.

Mark had phoned her from work. "I was thinking it would be nice to have a meal, just the two of us."

"I don't feel like going out tonight," Helen said. She was tired of the arguments that going out caused; she would rather just avoid them.

"Yes, well, I was thinking more of staying in."

"Okay, I'll give Louise her meal early." There was no emotion in her voice; there was nothing to be done other than dutifully agree with Mark's wishes.

"No, I've arranged for Louise to stay with your parents. They'll pick her up from school."

Helen could feel a surge of instant panic. She didn't want to be alone with Mark.

"But Mark—"

"No *buts*, Helen, make something simple, chicken I think, with a light salad – if you can manage that."

"Very well, Mark, what time?" She was feeling sick and the thought of preparing food turned her stomach, never mind actually eating with him.

"Seven, I'll bring home some white wine … and Helen?"

"Yes, Mark?" she replied obediently. Waiting for an insult – he could never resist an opportunity to degrade her.

"Even though we're not going out, could you at least try and make an effort with your appearance for once? The long black dress that I purchased for you last week would be acceptable."

The phone went dead. Helen looked at the time; it was nearly 3 p.m. Heading to the kitchen, she took the chicken breasts from the fridge and began preparing them. With the table set and the meal ready, she began the ritual of getting dressed. Helen was sitting in front of the dressing table: she left her hair down, blow drying it into soft waves. She was just starting to apply lipstick when the bedroom door opened. Helen let out a small gasp, "Mark, you startled me."

He walked towards her and placed a kiss on her cheek as he stood at her side. "You look lovely," he said, as he ran his eyes over her in appreciation.

"Thanks, I'll just go downstairs and add the dressing to the salad." Helen started to move but he grabbed her wrist.

"You look tired, Helen, what have you been doing today?" he asked, running a finger over her cheek.

"Just the housework and I had a slight headache earlier." He unnerved her, and now she could hear her voice quiver.

"You had a headache?"

"Yes, I took some painkillers, but the back of my neck is still sore." He moved his hands to her shoulders and began rubbing them.

"Tell me, Helen, what have you been doing that you look so tired?"

"Nothing, Mark, I told you."

"Strange to look so tired from doing nothing."

"Mark, it's probably my headache. They make me feel ill sometimes." She knew he was not going to believe her. It was always the same, and it was just going to be another night of sorrow.

"Are you sure, Helen, there's nothing you want to tell me?"

"I'm sure, Mark. Shall I go and put the dressing on the salad?"

"No, not yet, you do realise that I know when you've been up to something?" he said, pausing long enough to give her the opportunity to confess. "Who have you been with, Helen?"

"No one, Mark, please stop." She tried to move but he held her firmly by the shoulders.

Leaning in close he said, "You've washed your hair again."

"You told me to make an effort, Mark. Please stop, you're hurting my shoulder."

"Always you push me to my limits, do you enjoy hurting me like this, Helen?"

He reached out, grabbing the hairdryer from the dressing table, and quickly wrapped the cord around her neck. Helen began to struggle as the wire tightened round her throat, gripping the wire, she could feel her pulse pounding in her ears. Her fingers grabbed at the wire, unable to breathe, her movements became laboured, her arms and legs felt heavy, her vision narrowed, and then she could struggle no longer. She lost consciousness.

Helen opened her eyes, her hands instantly grabbing at her throat. The room was in darkness; at first she thought it was all a bad dream. She lay on the floor, listening. There was no sound other than her breathing. Struggling to her feet, she made her way to the bed. Reaching out, fumbling for the light switch, she sat for a long time at the dressing table, staring at the marks on her neck, too scared to leave the room. Mark didn't return to the room for the rest of the night. Helen was left alone with her fears. She sat on the bed all night, unable to sleep. It was in that moment she knew. His obsessions had no limits.

Charlie Selby handed her a tissue, to wipe the tears that were flowing freely down her face.

"You've done well today, Helen, I think we should end it there and next week we'll explore what you've told me today."

Helen simply nodded.

"Before you leave, listen to me carefully. Please don't hesitate to call the police. He will continue to harm you if you don't. Promise me, Helen, if he hurts you again you will call them."

"Yes, I will," she whispered as she left the room.

Helen walked home in a daze; all she could think about was Mark. He would go to any extreme to have her back. She knew sending Louise away was the right thing to do.

Work wasn't much better. She was unable to concentrate and Mr Wilson sent her home early. By the time Louise went to bed Helen had still not mentioned her plans to her. All night Helen tossed and turned and every noise sent fear racing through her body. Unable to stay in bed she decided that maybe she should pack Louise's things before it was time to wake her.

Eighteen

Louise opened her eyes, it was still dark. It was only 5.30 a.m. according to the clock, but even so, she could hear movement in the living room. Sighing, she forced herself out of bed. She wished her mum would try and get some sleep. Louise was aware that her mother had become more and more unsettled and was sleeping less and less. Every time she broached the subject, her mother tried to comfort her, giving her reassurance that soon things would be okay, saying she just missed Jerry and it was making her sad. Louise had to acknowledge the fact that since Jerry's departure, her mum was more miserable, but deep down she wondered if there was more to all of this. At this moment though, Louise was tired, she wanted to sleep but her mother padding round the flat was keeping her awake.

"Mum, it's so early, what are you doing?" Louise asked, standing in the doorway trying to stifle a yawn.

"Sorry, did I wake you, love?"

Louise looked at the pile of clothes on the couch. "Mum, please say you're not ironing, at this hour."

"Just packing some clothes. Listen to me, love, I know it may seem sudden but I think it would be best if you went to stay with Grandma for a while." Helen tried to speak in a positive, upbeat tone.

"Why are we going to Grandma's?" Louise was confused; there had been no mention of her in ages. She wasn't sure why they didn't talk, she just knew they didn't.

"Louise, try to understand. I need your cooperation. *You* are going to visit Grandma and Grandpa and I'm going to stay here. Come on now, do you want some breakfast?" Helen avoided eye contact and when the silence became too awkward and tense she made her way into the kitchen to fix something to eat.

Louise looked at her things spread out on the sofa. It looked as if she was going away for more than a few nights. Louise was frightened now. She could feel a rush of anxiety flowing through her body. There was a tight feeling in the pit of her stomach. She couldn't help but feel frustrated and angry, and her mum's silence was only making this feeling of sick uncertainty worse.

Louise noticed that her doll was among the things her mum packed. It was a little cloth doll that Helen had made, telling Louise it was a comfort doll, something to keep her safe when Dad was upset. Louise thought back to the night she got the doll. She was ready for bed and everything seemed fine, nothing unusual had happened and the evening was relatively quiet, for a change. Her mum went to the kitchen to get her some milk. It was their special ritual before bedtime; Helen always made her warm milk with honey. But as Louise pulled a chair up to the table to wait for her milk, she saw him – Timmy. He was lying on the middle shelf of the pantry, stiff, his face contorted and frozen in a wide-eyed, open-mouthed stare. Louise began to scream.

Helen ran to her, picked her up and cradled her in her arms. Mum and Dad had given Timmy to her for her fifth birthday. He was the cutest black fluffy kitten she had ever seen and she loved him dearly.

Much of what happened next was just a blur to Louise. There was a lot of shouting and crying. At some point, she remembered her mother's strong grip on her shoulders and the panicked look on her face as she said, in a loud, quick voice, "Get to your room, now!"

Later, when things went quiet, Dad came to her room. She never forgot what he said that night.

"Louise, are you awake?"

Louise was hiding under the duvet. "Yes, Daddy," she whispered. Louise wanted to pretend she was asleep, but she knew better.

"Louise, you are a big girl now, do you understand why Timmy had to die?"

Louise shook her head. She wanted to call out for Mum but she was too scared.

"Mummy has been very naughty again. She likes to hurt your daddy and it makes me very angry. Do you understand?"

Louise nodded, tears spilling down her face. Mark put his arm around her to comfort her.

"It's okay, sweetheart, Mum has hurt us both," he said kissing her gently on the cheek before wiping away the tears.

"Daddy had to kill Timmy to punish Mummy. She made me so angry. Mummy has to understand that what she does hurts us both." He smiled at her. "I would never hurt you, Louise, I love you. If Mummy would stop being naughty and love us we would be happy, wouldn't we?"

Louise knew never to disagree, so she nodded.

"Louise?"

"Yes, Daddy?" she sobbed.

"Stop whimpering now the cat is dead, do you hear me?"

"Yes, Daddy," she said, trying hard to hold back the tears.

Mark tucked her into bed and kissed her on the head. "Good girl," he said quietly before leaving the room.

It was later that same night, long after Dad went to sleep, that Mum slipped into her room and gave her the comfort doll.

"Louise, are you awake?"

"Mummy, is that you?" she whispered.

"Yes, love, it's me."

Louise sat up and threw her arms around her mum. Helen sat there for a moment holding Louise, stroking her hair.

Louise looked up at her mother and asked, "Did Daddy do that to your face again?" She could feel the tears starting.

"Are you okay, sweetheart?"

"Yes."

"Listen, I shouldn't be here," she said, holding her hand out. "I made her for you."

"She's beautiful." Louise loved the purple colour of her new doll.

"She's to keep you safe, you know, when Daddy is upset. She will cuddle you until Mummy comes to see you. I love you, Louise."

Kissing her on the cheek Helen whispered goodnight and left the room.

Slowly it dawned on Louise the reason why she had to go and stay with her grandparents. He had found them. Her throat felt tight, as if she was being strangled and she could hear herself screaming, although it sounded muffled, as if it were coming from a great distance.

Helen came running in and wrapped her arms around Louise, rocking her gently, stroking her hair. "It's okay. It's okay." They were both crying, locked in each other's arms, the full weight of their fears pressing hard against their hearts.

"He's found us, hasn't he?" Louise sobbed, still clinging to her mum.

"Yes, he has. But you've got to listen to me. You've got to do as I say and go to Grandma's. It's not up for discussion, love, do you understand?"

She was holding Louise by the shoulders and looking straight at her. "Now come on and help me finish getting your things ready, it's a long drive into the city and we need to get going." She couldn't stand to be hard with Louise, the look of confusion, fear and sadness on her daughter's face broke her heart. She didn't want to send Louise away but she had to. She had to be strong for both of them. If they ran away again he would only hunt them down. It was time to stand her ground and she couldn't risk doing that with Louise in the line of fire.

The drive into the city seemed to pass quickly. They were both silent, lost in their own thoughts. Finding a place to park wasn't easy, the city was a busy place. Helen purchased a single ticket for Louise.

"Mum, I don't want to go, please let me stay."

"No, Louise, it's not safe. You need to go." Helen was finding this situation difficult and if Louise persisted she might just persuade Helen to let her stay.

"I won't let Dad hurt you …"

"I'm not going to let him hurt me again, those days are over. But you've got to go to your grandparents so I can deal with your dad."

"How are you going to stop him?"

"I don't know just yet but I will. Come on, let's make our way to the platform. Your train will be leaving soon." They walked in silence through the station.

Just before Louise boarded the train, Helen said, "I love you, sweetheart." She leaned forward and kissed her daughter gently on the forehead.

"How much do you love me?" Louise managed a weak smile.

"To the stars and back." They hugged each other as if this would be the last time they would be together. "I'll phone every day, I promise," Helen assured her, gently nudging her onto the train.

"Mum?" Louise's voice was scared and uncertain. She was crying now.

"No, Louise. Go on now. I'll miss you."

The doors closed. The whistle blew. Louise was staring through the glass, she didn't want to leave. Her mother was protecting her, as she always did. The tears ran freely down her face now. She couldn't bear to wave, she was sure it was goodbye forever and that she would never see her again.

Helen ran alongside the train shouting, "I love you, Louise," and blowing kisses, until she could go no further. She stood there watching the train leave the station, her vision blurred by tears. For so long Helen had gathered her strength to carry on from Louise, now there was no one. But the important thing was that Louise was safe. Mark could never cause her pain, like the pain she felt now. But that was small comfort to her breaking heart, knowing, fearing she might never see her daughter again.

Nineteen

Helen stood there, still staring after the train long after it left the station. How long she was there, she was unsure. She didn't remember much of the drive home either. Saying goodbye to her daughter was the hardest thing she had ever done.

When she finally made it back home she parked the car and walked up the stairs to her front door. There was a long white box tied with a red ribbon propped against the door. Even with all the sadness in her heart at this moment, she couldn't help but give a little smile. She thought, surely, the box was from Jerry: flowers, a peace offering, maybe? Perhaps her life was going to change. Picking up the box, she went inside.

Helen headed for the kitchen. A strong black coffee was what she needed now. She filled the kettle and as it boiled Helen turned her attention to the box on the kitchen table. Who else would be sending her flowers but Jerry? Suddenly she didn't feel quite so alone. Helen opened the package. She gasped. It took a few seconds to register fully … screaming, she dropped the box.

As it slid across the kitchen floor, her eyes were fixed on the contents – a wreath in the shape of a cross with the words, *Our Daughter.*

Helen ran to the phone and dialled the only number that came to mind, the only person she could hope would care enough to help her. *Please let him be home,* she prayed. The phone seemed to ring forever before he answered.

"Hello." His voiced seemed strained.

"Jerry. It's Helen. Please, listen to me. Please. I'm sorry about everything. I'm sorry, please, can you come over?" Her voice was thick with urgency.

"I don't think that's a good idea." There was something in his voice; the possibility that he wouldn't come hadn't entered her mind until now.

"Please. Something has happened." She was sobbing now. She could hear the fevered pitch of her own voice. Panic was racing through her body, she needed him.

"What's happened?"

"I can't tell you on the phone. Please, I have no one else to turn to, Jerry." She could hear him sigh.

"I'll be there in a minute." He put the phone down.

Helen stared at the wreath. How did Mark know? A plea kept echoing through her head. "Please, God, don't let him hurt my little girl." Suddenly all that fear, pain, years of suppressed emotion was channelled in a rage, the likes of which she'd never felt. Where was he? She frantically made her way across the room to the window. Throwing it opened she screamed, "I'm here, you coward! Do you hear me? I hate you! You're not going to get away with this any more!" She kept screaming out of the window until there was a knock at the door. She was shaken by the sound of it. Closing her eyes she swallowed hard. She had to swallow her fear and face the possibility that it might be Mark here to answer her taunts. She took a deep breath, trying to compose herself: she could hear every breath, every beat of her heart, her legs struggled with each step as she made her way towards the door.

"Helen? Helen! Are you okay? It's Jerry." He'd heard her shouts and even though he was sceptical about the whole situation, he couldn't help being scared. He hoped, desperately, that she was okay.

"Helen, open this door! Do you hear me?" He was banging hard on the door now. It seemed like an eternity before Helen finally opened it. She looked so pale and her eyes were red from crying.

"Thank God you're here," she whispered, falling into his arms. She felt his strong arms wrap round her like a blanket blocking out the fear.

He held her, stroking her hair, whispering, "Ssh, it's okay, I'm here." Her smell was sweet. Despite everything that had happened, all the secrecy, all the lies, Jerry knew, in that moment, that he didn't ever want to lose her.

"What's happened? What's going on? I heard shouting." He was holding her now at arms' length.

She stood looking into his handsome face. She'd missed him so much and she knew, she simply knew, that the time for secrecy had long since passed. But as she opened her mouth to speak, she was at a complete loss for words. She had no idea where to begin and she wasn't even sure that she could make him believe her. She buried her face in her hands and began to cry again. All she wanted was to slide back into his arms. She missed his touch, his smell. Nothing seemed to matter now that he was here. Jerry closed the front door and led Helen towards the living room.

"It's okay, I'm here."

She pulled away from him. He could see the dark rings below her eyes. She looked totally drained. Whatever was happening was taking its toll on Helen.

"I can't take this any more, Jerry."

"Have you had another call?" Jerry asked, thinking of Mark's words and considering the possibility that he could be telling the truth after all.

"He's not going to stop and Charlie said I have to *make* him stop but I can't." Her voice was high pitched and she was shaking.

Jerry was confused. He had no idea who Charlie was. He gently slid an arm around her shoulder. He spoke gently but firmly. "You've got to calm down and tell me what's really going on. Come in here and let's have some coffee and relax for a little bit, okay? Then maybe we can get to the bottom of this, together." He sat her down on the couch. Without waiting for a reply he headed towards the kitchen. Now was not the time to tell her about Mark Waters. He could agree with Mark that things weren't right regarding Helen. You didn't need to be a doctor to see that, you only had to look at her.

Jerry glanced around the kitchen and shook his head. The work surfaces were crowded with an array of knick-knacks. There were all manner of salt and pepper pots bearing whimsical likenesses to all sorts of animals, various oven gloves that were completely impractical, and brightly coloured, mismatched ceramic serving pieces. He smiled. This was so typically Helen. She loved these things and even though he teased her about them, saying they were useless, she still wouldn't give in.

"What is it with you and this junk?" he'd once said, smiling and waving a snake-like pepper pot at her.

"It's not junk! Give me that back!" she said with a giggle, reaching out to grab it.

"What use are they? Some of their faces are ugly," he said and he pulled a face.

"You mean like the frog biscuit tin that croaks every time you open the lid, the same one you bought me the other day?" she asked as she stuck out her tongue and they both giggled.

"Hey, that's unfair! You made sad eyes at me in the shop so I had to buy it for you, and yes, it's totally useless like the other junk," he teased.

"They may be useless," she would say, "but they are cute."

He had to admit, they did liven up the dreary kitchen. She'd worked hard to add a personal touch to the flat, it was important to her that it have the feel of a home. He shrugged his shoulders and reached for the kettle. It was then that he saw the wreath; already it was showing signs of wilting.

Helen was standing silently in the doorway of the kitchen.

"Helen?" He looked up at her. Helen felt strange, empty, and indifferent to what was happening. A bizarre calmness washed over her.

"It was him. He sent it."

Jerry raised his eyebrows. "We're not back to this again, are we? It's probably a mistake; probably delivered to the wrong address."

"No, it's him, Jerry."

At this point Helen knew it was very unlikely that Jerry would believe a word she said. A weary expression settled on his face and she could tell that he was completely exasperated by all of this. But she felt as if she had to try. She had to at least tell him the truth and give him the opportunity to decide for himself.

"It's my husband. He's been watching me and he knows everything I do." She saw Jerry recoil: she couldn't utter words of comfort as she saw the pain wash over his tender face. Emotionally, she felt dead. She had one thing on her mind and that was Mark. He was here somewhere. If she could tell Jerry the truth, maybe there was a chance they could fight him together.

Twenty

Jerry had no idea how to respond. The woman standing before him seemed lucid. She was speaking in a calm, matter-of-fact way. But, nonetheless, it wasn't how she was saying it; it was what she was saying that simply didn't make sense.

"What do you mean, your husband?" Jerry was aware that his tone was more of an accusation than a question but Helen was unaware of the subtle change in his voice.

"My husband sent the wreath," she said, determined this time to try and convince him this was real.

"Helen, he couldn't have sent the wreath. Think about what you're saying for a minute." He was confused, he had just met her husband, or a man claiming to be, and yet he was challenging his existence.

"Please, just listen to me," Helen said. She wasn't going to be side tracked. She needed to make him listen, understand.

"Listen to yourself! It couldn't be your husband. He's dead, remember?"

All of this talk worried him. Jerry knew if Mark was right he would have to handle this situation with great care. Should he just go along with what she was telling him or was now the time to mention Mark? He felt completely unqualified to give Helen the kind of attention he suspected she needed and yet, with every fibre of his being, he wanted to believe her.

"Here, sit down and let's reason our way through this," Jerry said, reaching out to her, but Helen pulled back and she shook her head.

"I sent Louise to stay with my mum today and this is his way of showing me that he knows." Her thoughts were spinning wildly. She was struggling to make sense.

"What has Louise got to do with this?"

"You just don't understand, Jerry. I didn't have a choice."

"You're right, I don't understand any of this. You keep shutting me out, how could I possibly understand?"

"Well, listen to me. If you give me a chance to explain now! He's not like most people. He likes to play games like this, cruel games."

"I don't like to play games either, you know," he said, his eyes narrowing as a look of disgust ran over his face. As far as he was concerned, she had played emotional games with him during their relationship

"This is what Mark does. He wants to see me suffer. He's mad."

Jerry thought her choice of words was ironic. He looked down at the wreath. The thought flashed through his mind that, perhaps, Helen had sent the wreath to herself in order to substantiate her claim. It was entirely possible, too, that she wasn't even aware of doing it. He bent down, looking for a note, something – any evidence that would help him figure out what was going on; anything that would give him a reason to believe her. There was a gift-wrapped package nestled amongst the flowers of the wreath. Helen hadn't opened it yet.

"Helen, there's something here in the flowers," he said, bending down to retrieve the package. He handed it to her but she refused to take it.

"Aren't you going to open it?" Jerry asked, but Helen shook her head. Jerry began to unwrap it.

"No, don't open it! Please, Jerry, don't!" There was an insistence in her voice.

"Why, Helen? Do you know what's in here?"

"Of course I don't. Why would you say that?" she replied sharply. Her eyes were opened wide with amazement at his accusation, how could he think that?

"Then here, you open it."

He held it out to her again, but still she refused. Slowly Jerry finished unwrapping it. He looked at the box carefully before removing the lid. He could smell a strange odour.

"Oh my God!" He threw the package onto the table. His stomach was churning with the smell and the sight before him.

"What's wrong? What is it?" Her body was shaking as she took the few steps to Jerry's side. She peered into the package and immediately put her hand to her mouth and shut her eyes. She felt like she was going to be sick.

"That's it. Enough is enough! I'm calling the police!" Jerry made his way towards the kitchen door but Helen reached out and grabbed his arm. He swung round to face her.

"Wait! Please don't, they won't …" she paused, searching for the right words.

"They won't what, Helen? Either someone is doing this or not. Which is it?" he shouted, wrenching his arm from her grasp. He stormed into the living room. Running a nervous hand through his hair, he stopped for a moment to think. He felt he was walking on egg shells. He needed to call the police: all of this had gone too far even for him. Helen was in front of him, she reached out to touch him but he pulled back as if her touch would burn.

"Is it you, Helen, are you doing this? You'd better tell me now if you are."

"Me? No, I swear. No!"

"Well then, sit down; sit down and just be quiet for a minute. Stop being so ridiculous. You've got no option other than to involve the authorities. This whole game has to stop right here and right now!"

"Please, Jerry, I beg you, don't call the police."

He couldn't believe what he was hearing. He said, "Did you actually look inside that package, Helen? We need to call the police."

The odour circulating the room made her stomach churn. She didn't need to be reminded of what she had seen. "Please, Jerry, don't call them," she said, knowing that if Jerry wouldn't listen to her or believe her, then what use would the police be, never mind what Mark would do.

"Give me just one good reason why not, and don't dare say it's him." He was so angry. Maybe it was Mark he should be contacting, not the police.

"It will only make things worse, trust me. Please don't do this."

"Trust you? You can't tell me what's going on, but I have to trust you? Well, that's rich coming from you!" he yelled. Throwing his hands in the air he strode across the floor toward the telephone.

"I don't know what else to say to convince you." As she spoke he turned and looked straight at her.

He made his reply in a voice that was calm but strong. "Helen, I can't take this any more. I'm calling the police."

She hung her head. She knew she could not convince him. She would be unable to stop him.

"Hello, police station," said the dispatcher.

"I'd like to report an incident." *Incident*, he thought wryly, but he couldn't think of anything else to call it.

"Certainly, sir, may have the name and address please."

"Jerry Burns and we're at 3 Station Square."

"And the nature of the incident, sir?"

"We've received a package and the contents I can't begin to describe."

"There should be an officer with you in the next few moments, sir."

"Thank you." Jerry placed the phone down. There was an awkward silence as they stared at one another. Jerry shook his head. "Why are you testing me like this? You aren't helping matters, Helen, by putting on this act, by lying. You've made it impossible for me to believe you and that also means you make it impossible for me to help you."

"I know, but listen …"

"No, wait. No more until the police get here."

He took a seat on the edge of the sofa. He couldn't bring himself to look at her. He was thinking of Mark Waters. If she wasn't well he would have to be careful. The same questions ran over and over in his head. Why did she think her husband was alive? Was Mark telling the truth? He loved her so much why couldn't he believe her? He just sat there anxiously waiting. Fortunately, he didn't have to wait long.

The police station was situated a few doors away from the Rogue, Sergeant Campbell's favourite haunt.

"Sarge, do you think you should be drinking on duty?" asked Constable Brown. Drinking wasn't allowed on duty, even he knew that, but this man could drink.

"Listen, Constable, you're new here, nothing ever happens, and if it does we're in the right place, now drink your coke," he scoffed. "Bloody rookies think they know it all."

"But Sarge …"

"Don't *but* me, boy," he said as the crackle of the radio intruded.

"Sarge, come in."

"Go ahead, Janet."

"Got a call for 3 Station square, they got a funny package delivered. Over."

"On my way. Come on, lad. We'd better go and see, even though it won't be much." Campbell quickly finished his pint.

The young Constable watched, wishing he had never taken this job. He disliked Campbell immensely. The Constable walked in silence as Campbell made jokes about the contents of the package.

Twenty-One

The loud knock on the door made them both jump. Jerry went and opened it.

"Come in, officers." He led the two policemen into the living room. "Thank you for coming so quickly," Jerry said, extending his hand.

"Well, now, we thought we'd come straightaway. We were just down at the Rogue for a bit of refreshment and Janet radios and says you've got yourself an incident to report. There aren't many incidents to report around here, eh Dave?" The Sergeant pulled a face as he nudged the young Constable and laughed. His voice was loud and coarse. "Well, apart from the odd drunken brawl," the Sergeant said. He looked at Helen and grinned. "Hmm, sorry miss. I am Sergeant Campbell and this here Constable is … Tell the woman your name, lad. Bloody kids these days got no manners."

The young Constable went red in the face. He kept his eyes firmly fixed to his boots. "Brown, miss," he replied quietly. He was fed up with Campbell treating him like an idiot.

Helen felt sorry for Constable Brown, who looked to be in his late twenties, tall and skinny, with black hair. He was very shy, but then again Sergeant Campbell was a loud and overpowering man. Anyone would feel shy in his presence. Campbell was in his late fifties. He looked and dressed like a farmer rather than an officer of the law. He was an old-fashioned country bobby. There was nothing a quick clout round the ear or a good telling off wouldn't cure. He was about five foot ten in height and rather round and portly, with wiry slate-grey hair that was in need of a good brushing.

"Well then, where's this package, and what's so strange about it?" Campbell said, laughing slightly.

"I don't know how to describe it really."

"Well what are we waiting for, where is the bloody thing? I've not got all day you know," he said as he stuffed his hands in his pockets.

"Shall we go into the kitchen? I think it's best that you see this first," Jerry said. Campbell rolled his eyes, patience wasn't his best virtue. Jerry pointed to the package, he had no intention of looking at it again. "That's it on the table."

Campbell nudged Constable Brown hard with his elbow. "Well, go and look, boy," said Campbell sharply.

Constable Brown peered into the package. He put his hand over his mouth, the colour drained from his face and he ran for the front door and fresh air.

"Honestly, rookies!" Campbell went over to take a look for himself. "A bit pongy, ain't it?" he said as he waved his hand in front of his nose. He glanced into the package and pulled a wry face. "Who in God's name would want to send you such a thing?" He looked straight at Helen, who was standing in the doorway of the kitchen.

"Do you think they're real?" she asked.

"Won't know until we get them to the lab, miss, but my guess is, they're real." He reached for his radio. "Campbell here. Listen, Janet, call the doc and ask him to come around, looks like someone has sent Miss Mills a pair of eyes."

The radio crackled a bit. "Right, Sergeant, did you say eyes?"

"You heard right, eyes, yes. Now tell the doc. We need to send them to the lab, maggots and all." He grimaced at Helen. "I think we should go into the living room and take down a few details while we wait for the doc," Campbell suggested. Without waiting for a reply he turned and walked away.

The front door opened and Constable Brown came in, his face green.

"That you, Brown?" called Campbell,

"Yes, Sarge." Brown swallowed hard, trying to stop himself from throwing up. He'd never dreamed that he would see anything so disgusting. Those eyes sitting staring at him and the maggots crawling in and out was one thing, but the smell, it was rancid. How could anything smell that bad? He had been in the job six months and up until now it was alright, except for the Sergeant, but this – no way – that was it. Job or no job, he was going home to Glasgow. How he hated this job. He stood quietly in the living room hoping he wouldn't have to look in the package again.

Sergeant Campbell took a seat on the edge of the sofa. He was annoyed at Brown's display, nothing more embarrassing than a weak copper. Turning his attention to Helen, Campbell said, "Now, lass, what's the name?" He struggled with his notepad then threw it across to Brown. "Here, make yourself useful, lad." Dave picked up the notebook and waited. Campbell cleared his thoughts. "Okay, name in full, lass?" He nodded his head at Brown indicating he wanted him to take the notes.

"Helen Mills. Well, actually, it's Waters." Helen gave a sideways glance at Jerry but he showed no reaction.

"And you, Jerry, what's your full name, just for the record?"

"Jerry Burns, just for the record." He shot a look straight at Helen.

"Well, lass, how come you got a pair of eyes in a box?" The policeman looked at Helen. She cringed at the thought.

"It was him. He sent them. He's been calling me, watching me." She lowered her head. How could she expect Jerry to believe her now?

"Who's *him* when he's at home?" Campbell looked up at the ceiling. Why couldn't women just give you a straight answer?

"His name is Mark Waters," she said reluctantly, not wanting Jerry to find out this way.

"And …? You're going to have to help us out here. How is it that Mark Waters is related to you?" His comment was sarcastic. He always thought that incomers were trouble, and even though she was pretty, this incomer was trouble.

"He's my husband." Campbell was looking intently at her, her reply only served to convince him further that this woman was trouble.

"Miss Mills, you work at the Rogue, don't you?"

"Yes, you know I do. You've seen me there." She had certainly seen him, holding up the bar with Banes. Just her luck he was the local policeman.

"I thought you were a widow?"

"Well yes, but …" There was an awkward pause, she could feel Jerry's eyes on her but, taking a deep breath she continued, "My husband is alive." She looked across at Jerry. "That's what I've been trying to tell you, Jerry."

"So, what you are saying is that you lied about the death of your husband?" retorted Campbell. He felt quite good with himself, proving she was nothing more than a liar.

"Yes," she said. She was beginning to think that she was the one on trial.

"I see. So you're suggesting that your husband, who isn't actually dead, sent you the eyes and the wreath then? Perhaps you could explain why your husband might do such a thing?"

"Look, I've been seeing Dr Selby and …" In an instant she regretted her words.

"Dr Selby? You've been seeing *him* have you?" He began nodding his head, as if he was finally beginning to understand

"You don't understand, Sergeant"

"You're right, I don't. Your name turns out to be Waters and now your dead husband isn't dead."

"I can explain …"

"I suppose you're going to tell me now that Selby is helping you with your problems," he said, grinning at Brown and tapping his finger on the side of his head.

"No, it's not like that," she whispered. The look on Campbell's face said it all.

"Oh, no. I'm sure it's not. I'm sure it's not." Campbell's tone was patronizing and his expression was one of slightly irritated bemusement; but all the same, he was beginning to lose patience. The radio began to crackle.

"Sergeant Campbell, come in." It was Janet.

"Go ahead."

"Doc can't come. He says to put the eyes in something and bring them to the surgery. Over."

"Tell doc we're on our way." Campbell went into the kitchen and put the lid on the box. "We'll take these and we'll be in touch."

Jerry saw them to the door. At last, maybe he could get some answers. He turned to look at Helen. He felt so angry. But when she turned to meet his gaze he could see just how exhausted she was. She looked so fragile. Jerry didn't know whether to shake her or hold her. At this point he had no idea who or what to believe. He was sure of nothing but his heart told him he would be eternally sorry if he left her like this without at least trying to get some answers.

Twenty-Two

Helen was feeling very uncomfortable. Looking at Jerry she could tell he wanted answers. She felt exhausted and her mind was still reeling from Campbell.

Helen was sitting on the sofa now, remembering Campbell's condescending tone and how patronizing he was, all because she was seeing Dr Selby.

"Anything to drink in the house?" Jerry asked.

"Yes, there's some white wine in the fridge," she said with a half-hearted smile.

Right now he needed a drink. He could do with a whisky but the wine would suffice. He poured two glasses and brought one in to Helen. He sat beside her.

"So, you were married then, or are still married, I should say. Helen? Is that your real name?"

"Yes, that part is true. I ran away from Mark and came here

with Louise and changed my name." She drew breath.

He could see that this was difficult and Campbell's lack of sensitivity hadn't helped.

"Please, if you want me to help, I need to know the truth." He reached out and touched Helen's face. His touch felt warm and gentle against her skin. He was still here, he hadn't run. She knew he deserved to know everything. Helen was drained, emotionless, and defeated. Looking into his eyes she could see his pain, his torment. Wearily, she began her story.

"When I married Mark I loved him and I thought he loved me too. But he took that love and twisted it and manipulated it until it was nothing short of torture. He wanted to control me and he was cruel, even to Louise. I ran away and now he's found us." Tears were falling freely down her cheeks.

"Ssh, it's okay." He moved closer to her and gently slid his arms around her shoulders.

"You see why I had to send Louise away. He won't give up until he gets what he wants, and he'll hurt anyone who gets in his way."

"Tell me, Helen. I don't know why you sent Louise away."

She tried to control her tears, explaining this was going to be hard. "The beating started on the night of our first wedding anniversary. He promised that it would never happen again, but it did happen and it got more and more frequent. While I was pregnant with Louise, he kept me like a prisoner in my own home, never letting me out unless he knew where I was going and when I would be home. But most of the time he would come home from work and accompany me wherever I wanted to go. I was scared of him and I began to hate him. The thought of his hands on my body made my skin crawl. If I refused his attention then he would just take what he wanted in whatever way he desired, not caring if he hurt me. Then later he would cradle me in his arms and tell me that he loved me and desired me.

It was always my fault because I refused his advances, making him jealous. Mark was tormented with the idea of me in another man's arms."

Taking her hand he tried to find the words that would reassure her. "Just take your time, Helen, I'm not going anywhere." Jerry thought she was speaking with real conviction, he could see her pain. It made him wonder. Surely this was not all in her mind.

"After a while the beatings didn't seem to hurt the same, the hardest part was when he hurt Louise. He killed her kitten when Louise was only a child. Who in their right mind would do such a thing?"

Jerry held Helen tightly. He was finding this difficult to listen to. What he could not understand was why she sounded so genuine. Helen didn't want to look at Jerry. She hoped it wasn't too late to put things right and maybe, just maybe, he would understand why she had lied to him.

"Mark managed to isolate me from my friends and the one or two I had left thought that Mark could do no wrong. One day in desperation I told my parents about Mark, begging them for help. I'd tried once before to tell them, I should have known better. They didn't believe me then, why should they believe me now. I had to try at least, for Louise's sake. But instead of helping me, they called Mark to discuss it."

She paused, searching for the strength to go on. Her memory of that night was so vivid; it was as if she was reliving it. Mark was in a rage when he came home. "You bitch!" he screamed. "Get up those stairs, start filling the bath. *Cold* water." He lifted Louise from her bed and carried her, still half asleep.

"Mark, what are you doing? Please leave her alone." She grabbed his arm, holding on to him, begging him to let her sleep.

"Let me go, you lying bitch!" he screamed.

"Please, Mark, let Louise go back to bed, do what you want to me but please let her go."

He sneered at her, for a moment he said nothing, as if considering her words. "Sit down." His voice was cold, his eyes were dark, unfeeling, his face contorted with a rage she had never seen before.

"Please don't hurt her," she begged, sobbing for all she was worth. Louise was resting against her father's shoulder. Her eyes darted from her mother to her father. She was unsure what was happening but wise enough to stay quite.

"I said sit the fuck down!"

Helen's ear rang with the slap. In a moment she was on the floor. He plunged Louise into the freezing cold bath. A high pitched scream ran through the air, filling the house as the water washed over the child.

"Mummy, it's cold, please, Mummy, let me out, make Daddy stop."

Mark seemed oblivious to her constant screams. She repeated the words over and over until, finally, she just sat there shivering and whimpering.

"I pleaded with Mark but it was no good; he made me wait and watch. I was so scared of what he might do and at that point I would have done anything to help my daughter. Instead I did nothing; I just sat there and watched. Eventually he told me to call my parents and admit that I'd lied to them. Oh, Jerry, my life is a mess."

"It's okay," he tried to reassure her, but the truth was, he had no idea who to believe. He was confused, not thinking straight. He was torn between his love and his anger. He pulled her closer, his hands cradling her face and gently, he kissed her. Helen slid her hands under his t-shirt, running her hands along his back. Softly, he groaned in her ear and she began kissing him with a hunger. Aching with emptiness since he left, Helen only wanted him to love her. Jerry pulled Helen to her feet and, sweeping her up into his arms, he carried her through the room, placing her on the bed. She pulled him down towards her. She could feel his weight against her body and she could feel his passion. Letting their desire take them, they made love until they could make love no more.

When Jerry opened his eyes Helen was snuggled up beside him. Sitting up gently he looked at her, she seemed so happy and peaceful as she slept. Guilt flooded his thoughts. He had taken advantage of her, letting his own desire take control.

"I'm sorry," he whispered. He kissed her gently, got dressed and left. What had he done? He had let his passion get the better of him. He wanted her, but it wasn't enough. She had lied to him and that hurt. He could never trust her. He felt like a coward, making love to her and then leaving with nothing more than a note on the table.

Helen opened her eyes and reached out for him, but the bed was empty. She wandered through to the living room. There was a note. Quickly, she grabbed it.

> *Dear Helen*
> *I'm so sorry, this should never have happened. I find you've lied to me about everything, and possibly about the way you feel about me. I cannot deal with this. I need to think, please don't call me.*
> *Jerry.*

Jerry didn't want to believe that Helen had lied, but after being with her he knew that certain things about her were just not true. He would love her always, but they could not be together. He had kept Mark's visit from Helen and that made him a liar too. He felt like the whole night had been a sick test of matching and comparing stories. He didn't know who to believe. As he got near home, he remembered that he had a bottle of malt in the cupboard and tonight would soon be a distant memory.

Twenty-Three

Mark was standing in the woods, watching and waiting. The police had long since left Helen's flat, but Burns was still there. As Mark paced back and forth he kept looking at his watch. Yesterday morning he had been in this very spot when Helen and Louise left the house and he had not set eyes on Louise since, either she had returned home when he was at Burns' cottage or Helen had sent her away. Looking at the sky, daylight would soon be approaching. The air was still. He was aware of something moving in the shadows, it was a figure leaving Helen's – Burns, he thought. Containing his anger, he watched the figure disappear.

Approaching the steps to Helen's flat, he took a credit card from his pocket and slid it down the side of the door past the lock. The door clicked and he was in. Mark could not understand why she would want to live in this dirty flat instead of their wonderful villa in the outskirts of London. He explored the flat. Running his hand over the arm of the couch, he could smell a trace of her perfume. Opening a door, he glanced into the room. It was brightly decorated with nothing more than junk in his opinion. The posters on the wall made him cringe. Helen had obviously allowed Louise to do as she wished with the room. He would never tolerate this mess.

His thoughts were distracted as he noticed that the single bed was unoccupied. His suspicions were confirmed, she had sent Louise away, and there was only one place she would send their daughter. If all else failed he would collect Louise, forcing Helen home. Either way his wife would return to him.

Wandering into her bedroom, he saw Helen was fast asleep. There were clothes discarded on the floor. He lifted a shirt to his face and took a deep breath, letting her scent fill every inch of his imagination. He tossed the shirt down and started to leave. She had given herself to another man and she would pay dearly for this betrayal. He wanted revenge *now*. Fighting to control the hatred, he forced himself to leave, but on the way out he noticed a picture of his wife and daughter with Burns. He lifted it from the television. He would have happily smashed it, ripping this other man from her life, but instead, he went into the kitchen and placed it in the cupboard. He couldn't resist having a bit more fun, so he moved a few other things around for good measure. He heard stirring in the other room, so quickly and quietly he left, running down the steps and across the road to the woods.

Leaning against a tree, he sighed, there had been times when standing here had been more than watching; it had been a comfort, a feeling of intimacy with Helen, especially when he knew she was alone. But tonight was difficult; more difficult than he anticipated.

Mark could have stayed and watched Helen sleep, but he couldn't risk her waking up and seeing him there, it was too soon for them to meet. He had been at Weaver's Cottage when Helen called and he had cautiously followed Burns back to Helen's flat. It was hours ago that the police had left and Mark was still waiting and watching from the woods. Burns had been in there for a long time. Had he not impressed on this man the seriousness of Helen's mental state? What was he doing? Why hadn't he left? He had images in his head of them touching, making love, laughing. He tried to regain his composure. He needed to stay calm and focused.

Mark had not been able not resist entering Helen's flat when he saw Burns leave and, of course, it was obvious by the discarded clothes what they had been doing. Jealousy and rage were eating away at him. Standing in the woods he wanted to vomit, this time she could not deny the fornication, he had seen evidence of it with his own eyes. "Damn you, Helen," he cursed under his breath. Looking towards her flat he noticed that the lights were on. He waited and watched, composing himself before taking the phone from his pocket. Maybe now she would be ready to come home.

"Hello."

"Hello, my love, lonely are you?"

He was infuriated by her reaction, she had never before screamed at him with such disobedience. The smell of the Scots pine was stronger than ever. He could feel himself beginning to suffocate, his anger, his rage were choking him. He walked for hours before he regained control.

When Mark finally made it back to the cottage he sat down on the couch – 10 a.m. according to the clock on the mantelpiece. He was feeling much better. He would be glad to leave this cottage. It was, in his opinion, the pits of society. He took his mobile from his jacket and dialled a florist in the city.

"Hello, Adams florist. Can I help?" said a female's voice.

"I would like to order twelve red roses, please," Mark said in a soft, feminine voice.

"Certainly, madam."

He smiled, amused at his own deceit. "I would like to have them today if that's possible?"

"I'm afraid we would be unable to deliver today, madam."

"That's okay, my dear. I'll have someone collect them. When would that be possible?"

"We have roses in stock, I'll put them aside, so any time that suits you would be fine."

Excellent, he thought. He finished his call and went out to the car. He wanted to make one final check. He opened the boot and peered at the plastic bag. He gently stroked the dead cat. He would buy a box in the city, some blue wrapping paper would be nice.

"Sorry, kitty-cat, it was you or him and you lost." He shut the boot and got into the car. He was looking forward to the drive to the city.

The shop was pleasant enough. It was like any other florists, the bell above the door tinkled as he entered.

"May I help you, sir?" The shop assistant beamed at Mark.

"Yes, I've come to collect flowers for a Miss Mills," he said, smiling. He wanted her to remember him.

"Red roses wasn't it?" she said, making her way to the back of the shop.

"If you say so, I'm only the delivery guy," he shouted.

The girl returned with the flowers wrapped and handed them to Mark. "Here we are and there's a blank card. That's twenty-five pounds please," she giggled.

"There, thirty. Listen gorgeous, don't forget my receipt with the change, so this Mills lady pays me." Mark left with the flowers. A few moments later he was heading back to the car, pleased that his little shopping trip had been a success. He hoped Helen would like the wrapping paper he had chosen.

He was sitting just outside the village now, wrapping everything just so. He admired his own handiwork. How pretty, he thought – a cat with a bow.

Starting the car, he drove the next few miles singing:

> *Pussy cat, pussy cat where have you been?*
> *I've been to Strathburn to visit my queen.*
> *Pussy cat, pussy cat what did you there?*
> *I gave her such a fright I turned her grey haired.*

He stopped the car outside the pub and walked in. "Delivery for Miss Mills," he shouted.

There was an older man there and by the looks of it, he had been at the bottle.

"She's not here yet. Take it to her house." His words may have been slurred, but Mark heard the irritation in the man's voice.

"Can't. The delivery note says here. Go on. Take it, please mate."

"What is it anyway?" Mr Wilson's curiosity was awake.

"Flowers and a package, mate," replied Mark, trying to hide his annoyance. What was it with these villagers and there constant questions?

"For Helen, you say?" Mr Wilson was making a note to himself, the next time he saw that Burns bloke, he would be telling him to keep his love life out of his hotel, flowers indeed.

"Yep, if that's Miss Mills."

"Alright, I'll give it to her when she starts her shift tonight."

Mark left the pub with a smirk on his face.

Mrs Wilson came into the bar. "Have you seen Blackie? He's been gone all night."

Mr Wilson shook his head. That bloody cat, he thought. "No. Now go away, woman. I've work to do."

Mark was so tired now as he headed back to the cottage. He let himself in and went straight to bed. This was the first time in months he had felt he could sleep. He set his alarm on the mobile. The next thing he knew it was going off. He pulled himself off the bed and looked at his watch. Helen would be leaving for work soon. He grabbed his jacket and headed for the woods where he would wait and watch. Mark didn't have long to wait.

Helen seemed a bit anxious, he thought as he watched: walking down the street, stopping often and looking around her. He waited long enough to ensure she wasn't going to return before making his move. He didn't have much time now. He quickly made his way across the clearing and up the stairs to Helen's flat. Letting himself in, he headed for the bedroom. *Something warm tonight for my love,* he thought, *after the terrible fright you're going to get.*

He rummaged through the chest of drawers. Yes, he thought, blue was the right colour. With a smile he went into the living room and carefully arranged the pyjamas on the chair. He smiled a wicked smile and whispered, "All ready for you, my love, sleep tight tonight."

Twenty-Four

Helen stretched her arm out across the bed: the space beside her was empty. Opening her eyes she lay still for a moment, before swinging her legs out of bed. Putting on her dressing gown, she made her way into the kitchen. It was deserted.

Helen sat on the sofa clutching the note that Jerry left. It was 5 a.m. There was no point in going back to bed. Everything was a mess. She knew that she had lied, but Jerry had been different yesterday. Now that she was thinking a bit more clearly, he had seemed so angry with her before the police called and, if that was so, why had he come at all? Or, perhaps more importantly, why had he stayed? They had made love last night. She ran her hand up and down her arm. She could still smell him on her skin. She closed her eyes, trying to capture his warmth from last night. Looking around the living room, she sighed. This place was so lonely without Louise and without Jerry. Her heart ached, she loved him so much.

Something caught her eye as she sat there. She got up and made her way across the living room. Something was missing. She went over to the television. What was different? She thought, yes, of course, the picture of her and Jerry with Louise that had been taken on their picnic. She smiled, remembering the long walk they had taken, up into the hills.

"Mum, how much further do we have to go, before we can stop?" Louise had moaned.

"Just over there in the clearing, come on I'll race you," Jerry called and the pair took off. When Helen finally caught up with them Jerry was standing, looking across the valley and Louise was sitting on the grass, exhausted.

"Helen love, come over here and look at this view, isn't it breathtaking?"

Making her way over to stand beside Jerry, she could see a slight mist rolling over the tree-tops in the distance beyond the village. They stood in silence soaking in the tranquillity of the moment until Louise broke the silence.

"Mum, can we eat now? I'm starving."

Helen smiled, Louise wasn't known for her love of the outdoors.

"In a second, let's get a picture first, all of us together. This camera has a timer," Jerry said, grinning at them.

They all began laughing at Jerry's antics as he set the timer on the camera, making several attempts before succeeding. They had fun that day even though they got covered in midge bites.

She missed Jerry and Louise. She shook her head. Maybe he had taken it, but Jerry would not just take it, surely? She certainly wasn't going to call to find out.

She went into the kitchen and filled the kettle. She collected a mug from the draining board, added sugar to it and looked around for the coffee. She opened the cupboard door and, to her surprise, there was the photograph. A cold chill ran through her. How very odd, she thought, picking it up. She headed back to the living room and, after taking a good look around, she noticed that several things had been moved. She could feel the anger rise inside her. She knew he was angry but she couldn't figure out why Jerry would do this. She threw the photo down on the couch and headed for the bathroom.

The water beat on her shoulders as she stood under the shower and she felt the tension beginning to slip away. It was going to be a long day, but at least there was work. Things were a little tense lately with Mrs Wilson; she knew the woman definitely did not like her and she had no idea why, but as far as she was concerned a job was a job.

The telephone rang. Quickly she wrapped a towel around herself and ran to answer it, hoping that it might be Louise.

"Hello."

"Hello, my love, lonely, are you?"

She hated that voice. He was only at the end of the phone line, but still he could make her scared.

"Helen, love, what's wrong? Cat got your tongue?"

She could hear him laugh. She slammed the phone down. The phone rang again.

"Helen, my love, don't hang up. We could do this all day if you want."

"What do you want?" There was bitterness in her voice, why couldn't he accept the fact that she wasn't coming home? She knew the answer, his obsession wouldn't let him.

"Come home now, love, I promise things will be better. You know how much I love you." His voice had an empty chill.

"Never, Mark – do you hear me – never!" Her voice was trembling. She could hear its high pitch. As long as she had breath in her body she would never go back.

"Jerry doesn't love you like I do, Helen. He can't have you. I won't let him." The hatred was strong in his voice. "If I can't have you, Helen," he paused, "then no one else will."

The phone went dead. Placing the receiver down, she went over to the window. She knew he was out there, but where? She was becoming a prisoner again. She picked up the phone and started to dial Jerry's number. This time she would make him listen. He had to believe her. She put the phone back down as she began to realise what Mark had said. He had mentioned Jerry by name and the only way he could know about Jerry was if he was here in the village or, worse, if he had Louise.

She picked up the phone immediately and began dialling.

"Hello, Mum, can I speak to Louise?" She was so relieved when she heard her mother calling Louise to the phone.

"Hi, Mum! When can I come home? Are you okay?" Her voice was a warm delight to Helen's ears.

"Not yet, love, but soon."

"But I miss you."

"I miss you too. Have you seen your dad?" She didn't want to frighten Louise but she needed to know.

"No. Why, is everything okay?"

Helen could here the panic in her daughter's voice. "Everything is fine, don't worry. Now tell me, how's school?" She giggled, the relief was like a weight lifting from her shoulders.

"Mum, are you sure everything's okay? Have *you* seen Dad?"

"No, I haven't seen him, love. Tell me how school is. You're going to school, yes?"

"Yes, Mum. It's okay, but I want to be home with you, not here."

"Soon, love, I promise. You just have to be patient."

With their anxieties out of the way the pair chatted for a long time. They missed each other terribly.

The day passed slowly and Helen was unable to concentrate on anything. Looking at the clock, she realized it was finally time to prepare for work. She went through the motions of selecting a white blouse and black trousers. She had not lost all interest in her appearance; at least she would be tidy. Talking to Louise made her heart ache. She wondered if Jerry would be at the Rogue tonight. Deep down she knew he wouldn't. She hadn't seen him there since the night he walked out on her. Brushing her hair and tying it back, she took a final glance in the mirror before leaving the flat. She wasn't looking forward to work.

Helen entered the Rogue to start her shift. Her mind was elsewhere and the walk down had unnerved her. Mark didn't have her daughter, so where in the village was he? With every step she took, she looked around, feeling that at any moment he was going to appear. It was noisy as she entered the pub: at least something was the same.

"Helen, there's something here for you," Mr Wilson said, and by the sound of it he was plastered, as usual. He disappeared into the back store and returned carrying a box and twelve roses. They were deep red and the perfume was strong. She look at the flowers – searching, yes, there was a card. It read, "He doesn't love you." She placed the flowers down on the nearest table and looked at the box Mr Wilson was holding.

"Go on, pet, we all want to see what you got." He smiled at her. "Come on, love," he said as he started to help her unwrap it.

She slowly lifted the lid and stared in horror.

"What's wrong, love? Seen a ghost?" Mr Wilson looked in. "Jesus Christ! It's a bloody dead cat!"

Helen was crying. She sat down, still clutching the box, and that was where she stayed. She was still staring at the cat when the police arrived.

"Now then, Miss Mills, so you're collecting dead cats now?" Sergeant Campbell was not smiling. His look was one of disgust.

Helen just sat there staring into the box. He was never going to let her go, never.

Mrs Wilson approached Helen and handed her a glass. "It's brandy, dear, it'll help." She glanced into the box and screamed. "No, no it can't be!" Her screams were deafening.

Even in his drunken state, Mr Wilson was startled by his wife's screaming. "For God's sake woman! It's just a dead cat!" But his wife was pointing at the box and sobbing. He looked at her.

"It's Blackie! It's Blackie!" She turned to Helen. "That's my cat!" Mrs Wilson was taken away to lie down while the police took some statements.

Helen was left on her own. No one in the pub came near her, they just glanced over in disgust. They were all of the same opinion – this outsider was trouble. Helen saw the police making their way over, she was filled with dread at having to face Campbell again.

"Now then," he paused, "thirsty work this. Be a good boy, Brown, and get me a little light refreshment, eh?" The Constable shook his head, giving Helen an apologetic smile before heading to the bar.

"Right then, Miss, what's your name tonight?" He wasn't going to mince his words. He had to ask the question, he knew the answer would be a lie. After all he had already proved she wasn't trustworthy.

"Mills, Sergeant, if you don't mind," Helen said. Why was he treating her this way? She could feel everyone's eyes on her.

"I suppose you're going to tell me this is your husband's doing?" he asked, thinking that at least her lies were consistent.

"Yes, it could only be him." She was dutifully answering the questions, even though deep down she was aware that, no matter what she said, it would make no difference to this man's approach.

"Sending flowers to your wife is one thing, sending a dead thing is definitely different." The sarcasm in his loud voice was unbearable.

"Is there anything else you need to know, Sergeant?"

"Not for the moment, just don't leave the village just yet. Poor Mrs Wilson, you know she loved that cat, don't you?" He was condemning her. But he didn't care.

"Yes, I know," she whispered.

Constable Brown handed Campbell his beer. Campbell took one long drink and said, "Come on, son, let's go and see poor Mrs Wilson." He walked away, Brown followed slowly behind. He didn't want to be associated with Campbell. He was nothing more than a cantankerous old fool. The next hour passed in what felt like slow motion. Helen sat isolated but she could hear the whispers. They didn't even hide the fact that they were pointing the finger at her, laying the blame at her feet. Constable Brown appeared at her side.

"Miss Mills, why don't you go home? You don't look so good." He placed a hand on her shoulder.

"Is the Sergeant finished with me then?" She was nearing tears, she couldn't take much more.

"I'll deal with the Sergeant. You just go home."

She just nodded, collected her belongings and left.

Helen walked slowly home that night. No one uttered a word to her when she left. She opened her door and headed through to the kitchen. She came back to the living room with a glass in one hand and a bottle of wine in the other. She stopped dead in her tracks – there on the chair in front of her were her pyjamas all neatly laid out, but she hadn't done that. Or had she?

Twenty-Five

Jerry opened his eyes. The sun was streaming through his living room window. He flinched as he moved, every part of his body ached. His stomach churned as he saw the discarded bottle. Looking at the clock he realized it was 3 p.m. He must have passed out on the couch.

A shower helped ease his stiff muscles. But his conscience was still there. The bottle of whisky hadn't helped. Now, on top of everything else, Jerry had a hangover. He paced back and forth. What on earth could he say to Helen if he met her out somewhere? And in this place that was inevitable. It was not as if he could casually say, "Hey, sex was good last night, but don't come near me." What had he done?

He kept turning things over in his mind, weighing up what Mark had said and what Helen had told him. Helen had spoken of the beatings Mark had given her, the cruelty that both she and Louise had suffered, with such conviction. But who was telling the truth? Mark had come looking for him and told him about Helen's poor mental health. He was straightforward. Jerry thought he described Helen's antics as if he had done so many times before. What Jerry could not recall was any sense that this man was acting in the name of love, he just sort of said he loved her as an afterthought.

Grabbing his jacket, he decided a walk would help clear his head. The cool air was refreshing, but it didn't help. Maybe a pint would help instead.

Jerry made his way to the pub, timing it so that he would miss Helen. Sitting at the bar, he noticed there was a hum of excitement in the place. He couldn't have cared less, his thoughts were full of Helen.

"Didn't think you'd show your face in here tonight," Banes said, grinning at him.

"What the hell are you talking about?" Jerry snapped back. He wanted to be left alone.

"That lass you were seeing got sent a dead cat, here."

"Did you say a cat?" Mark's words echoed in his head.

"Hey, Anderson, tell him. Wasn't it a cat?"

Anderson nodded.

"Bet you're glad you dumped her, did you know she was screwy?"

"Helen? No." He could hear the folk in the bar, whispering, debating over the end of their relationship.

"They say she killed it herself," Banes said, carrying on the conversation, ignoring Jerry's hints to be left alone. Jerry said nothing more. Unable to sit any longer, he finished his pint and left quickly. Most of the crowd there made comments about his relationship with Helen and how it was a good thing that he was well out of it now. Like a coward, he went home without defending her.

He was trying to find a reason to believe Helen's story but she had lied and what Mark said supported that information. The episode in the pub finally sealed her fate. What had Mark said? *Ask her what she did to the cat.* Jerry was torn between his deep love for Helen and the plain facts in front of him. Helen was ill, and when this doctor got here and she received her treatment, he was going to be a faint memory to her. If he was lucky she would go home with her husband. Mark would be kissing her, holding her, making love to her. All Jerry would have left would be painful memories. He was going to lose her, no matter what. Even sleep escaped him, as Helen invaded his thoughts.

Helen looked at the clock on her bedside table. It was only 7.30 a.m. Dragging herself out of bed, she glanced at her tired reflection in the mirror. She looked as exhausted as she felt.

She had not slept well, tossing and turning most of the night. She could not remember leaving the pyjamas out and she couldn't remember moving things around in the flat either. All the windows were secure, the front door locked. There was no point calling the police. There were no signs of forced entry and no evidence to suggest that anybody else was involved. Campbell wouldn't believe her anyway. She was beginning to think she was mad – and going to see Charlie was not helping. Instead of making things better, therapy only seemed to churn things around – her emotions, her nerves. She felt like she was going mad. There were questions with no answers. Why had the frame ended up in the kitchen cupboard? Who had done this? The only answer terrified her – it had to be her.

There was a knock at the door. She nearly jumped out of her skin. Slowly she went and opened the door. The Wilsons were standing there.

"Come in, please." She tried to smile, pulling her housecoat closer, against the cool morning air.

"We'll not be coming in, you murderer!" Mrs Wilson screamed. "How could you?"

Mr Wilson patted his wife on the arm and said, "It's okay, love, leave it to me." He turned to face Helen.

Helen could only stare.

"I'm sorry, Helen, but under the circumstances we both feel …" he paused briefly "… that we have no choice. You're fired. I'll send what I owe you." There was only contempt in his voice.

"You killed my Blackie!" Mrs Wilson screeched, waving her finger in Helen's face. Mr Wilson gently led his wife down the stairs. She kept shouting "Murderer!" between her sobs.

Helen watched them as they walked away. It was the first time she'd seen them agree on anything. She shut the door. *Please, God, please say I didn't kill the cat.* What was happening to her? She grabbed her car keys. Not even dressing, she fled the house.

She was driving fast now as she left the village. She had no idea where she was going, all she knew was that she wanted to put as much distance between herself and the village as possible. There was a side turning, she took it, her driving erratic. Finding herself in a lonely country lane, she stopped. There was nothing now. Louise was at her mother's, Jerry was out of her life and Mark was hounding her. She was doing things of which she had no memory. The words echoed through her head, *You killed my Blackie. Murderer.* She placed her head on the steering wheel. Mark had won. She did not know what she was doing any more. If she died now nobody would care.

Jerry was standing in his living room, staring out the window. He struggled with sleep all night. He needed to resolve things with Helen. He had to come clean, tell her about the visit from Mark. Suddenly it struck him, if Helen was ill then she hadn't deliberately lied, or deceived him. None of it mattered, he still loved her and would always love her. Now he needed to talk to her about their future. The thought of Helen going home with this man was tearing him apart. He had to put things right. If she was ill, he wanted to help her, support her. He needed her to know that no matter how ill she was, he loved her. He wanted to be with Helen. He hoped it wasn't too late.

Jerry decided to drive; it was quicker than walking. He drove to Helen's, but there was no answer. He hung around for a while and then headed to the pub – maybe she was working extra hours. He soon discovered that was a bad move. The police had been in earlier in the day and the news was not good, at least not for Helen. He did not know what they had told the Wilsons, but Helen was not welcome there any more and he knew by the morning that she would not be welcome anywhere in the village. They would force her out.

He was feeling hungry. He realized that he hadn't eaten in the last two days. He ordered a sandwich and a pot of coffee. A while ago he had desperately wanted to see Helen. Now he had time on his hands, time to think and with every second that passed he felt his confidence slipping away. There was a very real possibility that Helen would reject him now. He was a fool to give Mark's words any credence. If Helen discarded him, he alone would be to blame.

Mr Banes was horrified by the news from the Wilsons. She was a good tenant and paid her rent on time but he could not let her stay in the flat now. The Wilsons were friends of his and she had killed their cat. God, who would do such a terrible thing to an animal? And would she stop at that? If he did nothing, they might not be safe in their beds. He wrote Helen a letter.

> *Dear Ms Mills,*
>
> *Under the circumstances regarding the Wilson's and the cat, I would like you to leave the flat, any time in the next week would be fine, just post the keys through the letter box of the flat when you leave that would be the best all round, don't you think?*
>
> *Yours*
>
> *D. Banes*

He gave her one week to vacate the flat. Which he thought was reasonable under the circumstances. He went to deliver the letter in person but there was no reply, so he posted it through the letter box. Maybe, he thought, the lass had some sense and had left. He would try again later, but next time he would bring the keys and check for himself. He'd pick the keys up after he visited the Wilsons. Maybe they would know if she had already left. And if she hadn't he would be able to reassure them that she wasn't welcome to stay in his flat.

Twenty-Six

Helen sat in the car sobbing. She didn't even have the guts to end her own life. She was feeling totally defeated. She started the car and headed home, parked and went up the stairs to the flat. She couldn't care less who saw her now. Slowly she opened the door. There was a letter on the floor. She picked it up and walked inside. At least it wasn't from him, she knew that much. Crumpling up the letter, she discarded it on the floor. They want me out, she sighed, now too tired to cry. She went into the bathroom and stripped. She felt numb all over, inside and out. She stepped into the shower. The water drummed on her back. At least there was one thing she could still feel, even though it was only water.

Constable Brown walked into the police station: he comforted himself with the knowledge that today he was working a half shift. All hope of a peaceful shift ended abruptly as he saw Campbell's face.

Sergeant Campbell was not in a good mood. This bloody woman was a pain in the arse, he thought, but he couldn't wait to tell her the good news that she was a psychopath. He had all the proof he needed now. He'd spent the last few hours collecting all the relevant information and was pleased with his efforts. But the thought of seeing her again was putting a damper on his day. Looking up from his paperwork as Brown entered the room he said, "Here, boy, read this."

"What is it, Sarge?"

"It's the report on that Mills or Waters woman, whatever you want to call her. It's all the facts. When you've read it we'll take a walk up there and tell her the good news, eh boy?"

Surveying the report, Brown shook his head. Campbell was beaming at him now, convinced he had solved the case of the dead cat. Constable Brown, on the other hand, felt that Campbell was an idiot and was wrong.

"Got a problem with the report, lad?" scoffed Campbell.

"Yes, sir, I have."

"Blurt it out, boy."

"Sarge, don't you think you should have gone to the florists, instead of just phoning them?" The report was full of obvious mistakes.

"Whatever for, lad? She told us who bought the flowers."

Brown scanned the report. "But according to your statement, you just asked who ordered them."

"And your point is what, Brown?" Campbell's mood wasn't improving.

"Were they delivered by the florist or were they collected?"

"Listen, I've been doing this job a hell of a long time, lad, don't tell me how to do my job!"

Brown wasn't going to give in. It just seemed to him that Campbell was determined that Helen was responsible for the last few days' events. "You haven't even been to see Dr Selby," sighed Brown.

"Don't need to, come on, lad, it's the nut doctor! You only see one of them if you're not right in the head." The more Brown thought about things, the more he was sure that Helen was being watched and someone had sent these things to her. With all his heart he believed that she was in danger. Campbell scoffed at this.

"What is it with you and this woman, lad?"

"I think she's in danger."

"A stirring in your groin and you cannae think straight, that's your problem, boy."

"It's not that, Sarge ..." He could feel the heat in his cheeks and Campbell noticed it.

"You're letting your hormones get in the way of your brain."

Brown didn't reply. Instead he was mulling things over: it sounded bitter, but before he left this place he was going to report Campbell.

"That's what women do to you, lad," he said.

Brown could not deny that he had warmed to Helen and given the chance he would be her lover, but it did not change the fact that she was in danger. Campbell, in that contorted head of his, had everything figured out. He was going to take great pleasure in telling everyone.

"Right, lad, let's get this over with." As Campbell made to leave the station, he noticed Brown lagging. "Well boy, are you coming?" he scoffed.

"I'm coming, Sarge," he said, slowly following.

The two officers stayed silent as they walked the rest of the way to the square. Brown had never felt as much loathing towards anyone as he felt towards Campbell.

Helen slid into a pair of jeans and a tee-shirt after her shower. Her stomach was rumbling; she hadn't eaten anything this morning. She padded around the kitchen. She was feeling more refreshed. She stared into her coffee cup, watching the liquid move as she stirred it. The toast popped up and Helen jumped. This was getting ridiculous – frightened by toast? What could be next? She sauntered into the living room and made herself comfy on the sofa, sipping her coffee slowly. The toast lay on the arm of the sofa: she didn't feel much like eating it now. She put her feet up to help her relax so she could think. There was a knock at the door. She struggled to her feet.

She sighed when she opened the door and saw Campbell and his constable. "What's happened now?"

"We need to discuss things with you, Miss Mills," replied Campbell, in his stern voice.

"Let me guess, you found a dead mouse and I'm the number one suspect."

The young Constable smiled at her and tried hard not to laugh, but the expression on Campbell's face was enough to make Brown to compose himself quickly. Helen thought that Brown was not a bad soul after all, but she could not warm to the Sergeant's rough demeanour.

"I suppose you'd better come in." She closed the door behind them and walked back to her comfy sofa. By the look of things she was not going to like what they were about to tell her.

"Well, Miss Mills, where do I begin?" He took out his notebook, consulted it, then launched into the most bizarre statement she had ever heard.

"The eyes came back from the lab and I am at liberty to tell you that they are sheep's eyes. But, of course, you already knew that."

Helen just sat there with her mouth open. How was she supposed to know they were bloody sheep's eyes?

"And we suspect that you got the wreath from the same florist." Campbell looked quickly at his note pad, "Adams florist in the city. We managed to trace this through the roses that you purchased there. We have confirmed this with the sales assistant." He was rather pleased with himself. He couldn't prove that Helen had killed the cat. "Anyone seeing a psychiatrist needs help," he paused, choosing his words, "killing the odd cat and sending it to yourself with the odd eye or two is your own business."

Helen managed to gather her thoughts enough to interrupt him. "I didn't send them." That was one thing she knew, she never went into the city.

"Well, that's what you say, but obviously I know you did." The annoyance in his answer was obvious.

"Excuse me, Sergeant," Helen said, anger rising in her voice.

Campbell held his hand up to silence her. He wanted no more interruptions. "I suggest, Miss, that you leave Strathburn as soon as possible." His tone was stern.

"What? But I haven't done anything wrong!" She hadn't expected that. Why should she leave?

"Take my advice: go before I find something to charge you with." He stuffed the notebook in his pocket. As far as he was concerned the matter wasn't open for discussion.

"Sarge!" Brown shouted. He couldn't believe his ears. Campbell had overstepped his boundaries now.

"Shut up, Brown," he growled. He threw him a look that meant business. "You're not wanted in this village, do I make myself clear?" He turned to leave but Helen jumped to her feet.

"Is that it? You can't just walk away."

"I can, Miss, and I will."

Helen tried to reason with Campbell and explain that she had done none of this. "It was him! I swear, it was Mark!"

He was infuriated now. She wasn't going to be reasonable.

"May I remind you that you have two surnames, neither of which I believe, never mind your cock-and-bull story about your husband, if you have one, being responsible for any of this." He was glaring at her. "Goodbye ,Miss Mills!" he said, slamming the door as he left.

The young Constable lingered behind. Unsure of what to say to Helen, he took his notebook from his top pocket, scribbled something down and handed it to Helen. "This is my home number and my mobile. If you ever need my help, call me." He smiled at her and gently touched her arm to reassure her.

Taking the paper from him, she smiled weakly and said, "Thank you."

"If it's any help, I do believe you." And with that he said goodbye and followed after Campbell.

Walking back to the police station was difficult: every time he looked at Campbell, who seemed so pleased with himself, Brown just wanted to punch him. After the incident with the package, Brown had turned in his notice and Campbell had accepted it. In another half hour Brown's shift would finish and he had only another twenty-one days to go, and counting, and it wasn't coming fast enough. Campbell was just as happy for Brown to leave, in fact he couldn't wait. He just hoped that they wouldn't send him another rookie that he couldn't tolerate.

Twenty-Seven

Helen stared at the front door after the police had left. Things were going from bad to worse, everything was spiralling out of control and she couldn't stop it. The walls were closing in on her – work, Jerry, and now this, it was the final straw.

Helen could not believe it. In one day she had been accused of murder, had lost her flat and been called a psychopath. She had no choice but to leave now. She made a quick call to her parents.

"Hello, Mum, it's Helen," she said, her voice flat, lifeless.

"Helen, what's wrong?"

"I don't know where to start, Mum," she said and started to cry.

"Helen, we know, Louise has told us all about Mark. I'm sorry we didn't believe you. We're both so very sorry, please forgive us." She held her breath, hoping it wasn't too late to make amends.

"Mum, it doesn't matter any more. Can I please come home, just for a while? I've nowhere else to go," she said in between the sobs.

"You know you can, Helen. We have so much to make up for."

"Thanks, Mum."

"Listen, love, when are you coming? Your father and I could come and get you."

"No, I have something to do first. I'll call you later and let you know when I'm coming. Tell Louise that I'll see her soon." Putting the phone down, she felt relieved. Her parents actually seemed delighted that she was coming home. At least for a while she would have a safe place for Louise. Feeling too tired to run any more, she would pack some clothes and Banes could do what he liked with the rest. Her skin was crawling all over and she felt dirty. Campbell had said horrible things, and her skin felt like he had touched her and it was foul – she had to go for another shower.

Drying herself, she felt clean at last. She was slipping into her housecoat, thinking about what to pack, when the phone rang. Wandering through to the living room, she thought of Jerry. Maybe she would tell him. *Better still*, she thought, *I'll write and that way it won't hurt as much if he doesn't answer.* She reached out for the phone and then she froze. The phone stopped ringing. Mark was sitting in the armchair with his mobile in his hand.

"Hello, my sweet Helen." He was sitting near the door. There was no other way out of the flat.

"Get out!" She did not approach him, that wasn't safe. Besides, she couldn't move if she tried. She was frozen to the spot.

Mark got up from the chair and walked towards her. "Helen, Helen, Helen." Slowly he reached out and touched her face, running his fingers down her cheek and across her lips. "I've missed you so much, love."

"Leave me alone, Mark," she said nervously, taking a step back.

"Don't I get a welcome home kiss, darling?" His tone was gentle.

"When hell freezes over," she spat. It no longer mattered what she said, he would do what he wanted. He leaned over and tried to kiss her. She moved her head and Mark lashed out with his hand. Her ears rang with the slap.

"Tut-tut, Helen, that's no way to greet your husband. Shall we try that again?" His tone was sarcastic. She felt his finger dig deeply into her arm.

Running his other hand across her neck he whispered, "Your skin was always so soft, I've missed touching you." Cupping his hand around her breast, massaging it softly, he said, "This is what you like, isn't it, Helen?"

"I hate you, Mark," she said, her voice barely audible. There was nowhere to run.

"Bitch, you wouldn't say that if I was him!" he said. He grabbed her hair and pulling her head to the side, he ran his tongue over her neck, whispering softly in her ear, "Let me show you what you've missed all these months." He brought his mouth down hard on hers, there was no affection, only hatred. She was struggling but he was too strong: pushing his leg between her thighs, he forced her up against the wall. Just then there was a knock at the door. He tried to ignore it. He hoped whoever it was would go away but the knocking persisted.

Mark grabbed Helen and dragged her to the door. He said, "Get rid of whoever it is!" He twisted Helen's arm.

She opened the door slightly. She wanted to scream out for help but instead she heard herself say, "What do you want?" Her voice was trembling. Her eyes were wide.

Constable Brown realised that something was wrong. He had to think quickly. "Banes said you have another leak."

He didn't take his eyes off her, hoping that she would let him in. Helen was mouthing the words, *help me*.

"No, it's alright. There wasn't a leak after all."

"Are you sure? It would only take a moment to check." Brown was nodding, letting her know he understood.

"No, I don't need you to look, thanks anyway." She hoped he would go, there was no way she could let him in.

Mark was tightening his grip. She said goodbye and closed the door. He held her up against the door. Again he leaned over to kiss her. Determined to finish what he had started. She pulled her head away. This time he hit harder, knocking her to the ground. She was dazed. Grabbing her, he turned her on to her stomach, his knees on her back. She tried to struggle but he was too strong. She couldn't breathe now, he was squashing her, and then the familiar blackness came.

Mark knelt over her. "Helen, why do you always have to be so difficult?" he whispered. Picking her up gently, he placed her on the chair. Stroking her hair, he sighed, she was so beautiful. "I love you, Helen, only you." Mark bent down and brushed his lips against hers. He noticed some packing tape on the mantelpiece. Lifting the tape he smiled: this would be useful. Mark sat down, watching her, admiring her. It was hard not to get distracted, but he reminded himself why he was here – no matter how much he cared, she had to be punished.

Helen began to stir. When she opened her eyes she found that her hands and feet were taped and she was sitting on the chair. He was standing over her, smiling. He gently ran his hand down her face and onto her breast. She tried to struggle and he just laughed. He could feel his anger rising.

"You wouldn't pull away if it was Burns, would you? Well, he's not here to help you now, is he?" he laughed. "You slut, I knew it all those years, every word out of your mouth was a lie. But I can forgive you, Helen. I love you. All you have to do is come home." He was trying to control himself, but she was pushing him away, baiting him with her defiance.

"Never, Mark, do you hear me? Never!" She would rather die than spend the rest of her life with him.

"Bitch! Whore!"

Pain ran through her jaw. She could taste the blood in her mouth. Leaning over her, he kissed her cheek. He loved her and she was pulling him apart, rejecting him like his mother had, in favour of another man.

"I love you, Helen, don't you understand? Please, don't make me hurt you any more," he pleaded with her.

"This isn't love, Mark. You don't know how to love."

The words echoed inside his head, the pain was becoming unbearable. "Say you will come home and it will stop."

She shook her head. It would never stop. Mark went into his pocket and took out a pack of cigarettes and a lighter and put them on the table. Then he produced a small can of lighter fuel. He was determined, if he could not have her no one else would. He lit a cigarette and taking a draw he blew the smoke in her face.

"I will ask you again. Come home."

She looked at him and shook her head. She was too scared to speak. Mark stared at her for a moment. All he could see in her face was contempt for him. He could deal with anything, but not her hatred. He understood in that moment that she didn't love him. Something snapped inside as he pushed the lit cigarette into her soft flesh. She felt the pain on the top of her thigh. It was burning deeply. As he twisted the cigarette around, she started screaming. He laughed as he placed his hand tightly against her mouth. When the screaming subsided he took his hand from her mouth and reached over for the lighter fuel, sprinkling a small amount on the edge of her housecoat, before spreading the rest liberally over her body. He took his lighter and lit it.

"All you have to say is yes." He held the lighter closer. Helen tried to push back into the chair. Slowly, he held it close to her face then lowered his arm, tracing down her body to the edge of her housecoat.

"I hate you," she whispered.

Mark kissed her forehead.

"Please don't ..." she begged, her words trailing.

"Goodbye, my sweet Helen." She had given him no choice now. He held the lighter to the edge of her housecoat and stood back to watch. She opened her mouth and screamed.

Twenty-Eight

Constable Brown finished his shift and changed out of his uniform. He was ready for a drink. After the way Campbell had behaved towards Helen, he needed one. But on the way to the Rogue he changed his mind and instead he went to Helen's.

As he spoke to her on the doorstep, he noticed the red welt on her face. Her eyes darted back and forth like a frightened rabbit.

Afterwards, Dave Brown stood just a few yards from Helen's flat. Taking out his phone, he called Campbell. "Sarge, I'm outside Helen Mills' flat, there something's wrong. I think you better get over here." He was trying to keep his voice down.

"Leave it be, lad, she's trouble," Campbell said, sounding like he didn't care.

"I don't think you understand – you need to get your arse over here now, Campbell, she's in trouble." He had nothing to lose now; he had already given his notice. But Helen had everything to lose.

"Listen here, Brown …"

"No, you listen, someone has her in the flat," he said, trying to make him understand there wasn't much time.

"And how do you know that?"

"I've just been there. Now get over here or so help me I'll report you!" he yelled.

"Keep your hair on, boy, I'll be there."

Brown waited outside the flat. He could hear muffled screams from inside. He paced back and forth, thinking that it would be stupid to go in alone. He might make it worse for Helen. But if Campbell didn't hurry up he would have no option.

Meanwhile, Jerry was sitting at the pub, staring into his pint, his sandwich long disregarded. He wondered if he should go back and see if Helen was home yet, but he did not know what he was going to say to her. His thoughts were interrupted by Anderson who sat beside him. This man was a gossip and could be nasty with it. Jerry disliked him. He looked at Anderson.

"What do you want? Is there something about Helen on your mind?" He was being sarcastic, but he was horrified by Anderson's reply.

"I was just thinking about all that trouble your lass has got herself into," he said, nodding. Since the night with the cat Anderson had been turning things over in his mind.

"What about it, Anderson?"

"There's been a strange chap staying at my cottage, some writer or other called Waters," he said, still nodding his head. After all, strange things had been happing in the village since that Waters chap had arrived.

"How long has he been there?" He had Jerry's full attention.

"About three or four weeks, paid up front, three months' rent. Funny character, really interested in your and Helen's movements. I've seen him on many occasions, standing for hours in the clearing, just across from Helen's flat."

Warning bells rang inside Jerry's head. He knew immediately that Helen had been telling the truth the whole time. He got to his feet. By the time he got to the pub door he was running. The adrenaline was racing through him; there was a fluttering in the pit of his stomach. He knew that she was in danger.

Running now as fast as he could, he could see Brown standing just outside Helen's flat. His heart sank. A few seconds later he had Brown by the shoulders.

"Is Helen alright?" He was frantic, shaking Brown as he spoke.

"I've seen her, she's okay for the moment," Brown said, pulling himself free of Jerry's grip.

"What do you mean, for the moment? She was telling the truth all this time! We need to help her." He couldn't understand why Brown was standing there doing nothing. He made his way towards the flat.

"Calm down, this won't help Helen. Campbell's on his way," Brown said as he grabbed Jerry's arm, stopping him from going up the stairs.

"That buffoon? We need to get up there now!" he yelled.

"No, we need to wait: we might endanger Helen's life." Brown thought he was going to have to restrain Jerry.

The pair stopped as a penetrating scream pierced the air. Jerry couldn't wait now. He ran up the stairs and put his foot to the door. It swung open with the greatest of ease and in a second he was in the living room. He paused in horror at the sight before him.

"NO!" Jerry yelled, as he threw himself at Mark. It was too late, flames rushed up Helen's housecoat, engulfing her. Mark was knocked off balance, landing on the floor. Jerry grabbed Helen and threw her down on the floor, trying to roll her to extinguish the flames.

Mark recovered himself quickly, taking a few strides he yelled, "Get away from her, you bastard!"

Jerry felt a vice grip on his shoulders as he was yanked to his feet. Mark's punch was direct, knocking Jerry off his feet and sending him crashing into the coffee table. Jerry hadn't expected this man to have such strength. He was like a man possessed.

Hearing Jerry's yell, Brown rushed up the stairs to the flat. Seeing Jerry on the floor, he ran at Mark, tackling him from behind. Mark struggled, tossing from side to side. Brown wasn't sure how long he could hold onto him.

"Get Helen!" Jerry shouted as he struggled to his feet.

Brown let go of Mark and as he passed the sofa he lifted the jacket that was there, quickly threw it over Helen and made sure the flames were definitely extinguished.

Jerry and Mark were struggling violently now. No matter how many times he hit the bastard, Mark just kept charging at him. He was driven now by hatred.

Campbell came running in, puffing and panting. He went straight to Helen. Seeing her filled him with fear. He was responsible, if only he had listened. He began to look around for anything that he could use to cut her bindings.

Mark had Jerry on the floor. With one hand round his throat, he was sitting across him, using his weight to hold him down. He wanted his revenge on Jerry. If he was gone, then Helen would come back to him. He snatched a lamp and raised it above his head: he was going to finish this bastard once and for all. Just as he was about to bring it crashing down, Brown dived at him, sending the lamp sliding across the floor. Mark was on his feet. Brown tried tackling Mark from behind with little effect: he swatted the Constable from him like a bug and headed out the door. Brown followed him.

Banes was driving into the village. He was in a hurry to get home. Having stayed longer at the Wilsons' than he'd intended, with one or two whiskies under his belt, Banes smiled. She was an old car, but this baby could move when she wanted to. He leaned over and, taking his eyes from the road, he patted the dashboard. Out of the corner of his eye, he got a glimpse of something. Slamming his foot on the brakes, he could feel the car shudder as it came to a stop. Banes sat and stared, wanting to be sick but unable to move.

Constable Brown came running down the steps. He heard the screeching of the brakes, and his eyes were drawn towards the noise. There was nothing he could say or do as he watched Mark's body fly up into the air and come back down to rest on the bonnet of the Ford Cortina. Blood splattered from his mouth, there was no other movement.

Brown leaned into the car and spoke to Banes.

"Are you okay, mate?" He could smell the alcohol on his breath.

"God, I didn't see him, he just ran out." Banes began to sob.

"Just stay in the car for the moment, Mr Banes." Poor bastard, thought Brown. He took out his phone and dialled 999. All he could do now was wait.

Jerry had stayed in the flat. He was more concerned about Helen. Campbell cut the tape that was binding her and, leaving Helen with Jerry, he went outside to see what was going on. Jerry knelt down beside her. She had burns. She just lay there silently. He was holding her face, kissing every inch of it.

"Thank God you're alive," he said. When he first entered the flat and saw the flames he'd thought he was going to lose her forever.

Everything happened very slowly after that. He was in a daze. There were lots of flashing lights, sirens, people coming and going, asking lots of questions. It all seemed unreal.

Jerry would not let Helen go to the hospital without him. He sat in the ambulance, holding her hand. "I'm sorry,

I should've listened to you, Helen." He blamed himself. He was responsible for her injuries. God, she could have died. "Helen, please say something, anything." But there was no sound. "Please forgive me, say you forgive me." Even if she screamed at him it would better than this deadly silence. "I love you, Helen."

He so badly wanted her to forgive him, but Helen stayed quiet, she had been through so much. Was it ever going to stop? Unaware of any pain from her injuries, emotionally she felt she had gone to hell and back. She was vaguely aware that Jerry was at her side. She could feel him holding her hand and hear his words of love as he asked for forgiveness, pleading with her. Helen was unable to look at him. *Funny*, she thought, *they all want to be forgiven*. Turning her head away from Jerry, a tear escaped from the corner of her eye and gently trickled down her cheek. Helen decided that, if this is what happens when somebody loves you then she would spend the rest of her life loveless.

Twenty-Nine

The next thing Helen remembered was the bright lights of the hospital. She was in a room. She looked around slowly. There was a drip in her arm, and as she tried to move there was a wave of pain.

Constable Brown put his hand out and rested it on her shoulder, shaking his head at the sight of her injuries. Her beautiful face was bruised and swollen, and there were burns on her legs and hands. He spoke gently.

"Its okay, Helen, you're safe. It's over." He had been there for a long time – he didn't want her to wake up alone. If only he had stood up to Campbell, things could have been very different. Helen smiled weakly at him and drifted back into unconsciousness. The medication they had given her was doing its job. Brown was relieved when the doctors said she would make a good recovery, at least physically. The burns to her legs were nasty, but would heal in time. The burns to her arms were superficial and there were no broken bones, which surprised him, she looked as if she had taken quite a beating. They would give her painkillers for the next few days, as she would be very tender.

Twenty-four hours later, Helen was awake. Her legs hurt the worst and the doctors said they would scar, but she didn't care at the moment. She was alive and that was all that mattered. The door opened and the nurse popped her head in.

"Up to having a visitor?" She smiled warmly at Helen. "He's been here all night." Helen's face paled. He had been there all night. Mark was still there after all this. He was still here, here to take her home. The nurse saw her expression and came into the room.

"It's okay, I'll just tell Mr Burns that you're not up to visitors yet."

"No, it's okay. I'll see him." The relief washed over her now, remembering vaguely what the nice Constable had said. It was over. She hoped that she hadn't dreamt seeing Brown.

Arriving at the hospital, Jerry could only watch as they wheeled Helen away from him. He had tried to follow her but he had been stopped. The doctors insisted that Jerry be checked over before he went anywhere.

"Let's have a look at you, Mr Burns," the young doctor smiled.

"I'm fine. Where's Helen? Where have they taken her?" He needed to be with her. He didn't want her out of his sight again.

"The doctors are with her now. That's a nasty bruise on your face," the doctor said, leaning over to look.

"I want to see Helen now!" demanded Jerry.

"Once we've checked you over and not before, Mr Burns." Resigning himself to the fact that he wasn't going to see Helen without a check-up he gave in.

"Let's get it over with then," he sighed. He only had a few cuts and bruises. It might take a few days for the swellings in his cheek and top lip to go down, but apart from that he was fine. Since then he had sat with Helen until the staff chased him from the room. Not wanting to leave her, he stayed outside in the corridor, hoping that when she woke up, she might understand enough to forgive him for not believing her. Who was he kidding? He, and only he, had put her in danger. If only things had been different. Walking into her room now, Jerry was prepared for the possibility that she might hate him. After all, he had done everything to warrant her mistrust and hatred.

He popped his head around the door.

"Hello, Helen. Can I come in?" He paused at the door, waiting for screams of anger, which he so rightly deserved.

"Yes, please do." She tried to sit up more, but it was too painful. Jerry rushed to her side.

"Helen, try not to move."

She looked at him, unable to find any words. Wondering what he was thinking of her now and scared that the knowledge of Mark would be between them for ever.

They sat for a while, unsure of what to say to each other. Jerry decided to be honest with her.

"There's something I must tell you. Mark came to see me. He told me that you were mentally ill."

"And you believed him?" Helen knew she had not helped by hiding her past. But knowing that he had believed Mark left a nasty taste in her mouth.

"Some of the things he said just seemed to fit." He was shifting back and forth on his feet, squirming on the spot. Every time he looked at Helen, he knew how badly he had let her down.

"When did this happen?"

"The day you got the wreath, he was there when you phoned." He looked down at his feet; he couldn't bear to see the look on her face. He was full of pain.

Helen realised he was as much a victim of Mark as she was. "I should have been honest with you, Jerry."

He understood now why she hadn't, but at the time it had been different. Mark had sounded so believable and when the police came around and he'd discovered that Mark was really her husband, and alive, well, he'd felt betrayed and hurt. Just like the night he found his girlfriend and his best friend together. But one thing was for sure, he would buy Anderson a pint the next time he saw him. It was him that had made Jerry realise that she had been telling the truth.

"It's okay," Helen said. She knew what Mark was capable of, how he charmed everyone he met.

"No it's not okay, look at you, Helen," he said, tears forming in his eyes as he looked at her swollen face.

"This is what Mark does – he manipulates people. He sounds so plausible." Even her parents hadn't believed her when she had tried to tell them what was happening. It was only when Louise went to stay with them that they discovered the truth about Mark and what he had done to them both.

"But Helen, you—"

She interrupted him. "Don't let him torture you." She knew that was what would happen if he kept thinking this way. There was only one person to blame and that was Mark. There was one question burning at the back of her mind. She asked, "What's happened to Mark?" She hadn't seen him and she needed to know where he was.

Jerry had no answer to this. He had not given Mark a second thought in that respect, and could not recall even seeing him after he fled from the house. He had seen Constable Brown since then but he had made no mention of Mark either, although he did mention Sergeant Campbell – by the sound of it he had been suspended from duty until after the enquiry. Their conversation was disturbed by the doctor.

"Miss Mills, or rather ..."

She interrupted him. "Mills is okay," she said, tired now with all this.

"It's about your husband."

She held her breath. This was what she had been waiting for.

The doctor began to explain. "Your husband is stable. Not many people survive that kind of impact from a moving vehicle."

"He was hit by a car? Where, when?" Helen was confused, realised that the last thing she actually remembered was the flames, the rest was just a blur.

"Outside your flat, I believe, the police will have the exact details."

Helen just nodded. She was still trying to decipher the glimmers of memory.

"His recovery will be a slow one, but with help he will make good progress considering that he is paralysed from the neck down." They both just stared at the doctor. "When you're feeling up to it, I'll come back and discuss the care that your husband will need when you take him home."

Helen was unable to say anything. She thought that he would be behind bars, not this, she had not wanted this. He was going to be condemned to his own hell and for a brief moment she felt pity and compassion for Mark.

Jerry was listening to the doctor intently. Had no one told this fool what Mark Waters had done to Helen? It was then that he realised that Helen had said nothing. Surely, he thought, not after everything that's happened? It was then that Jerry felt he had no place here. He stood up, placed a kiss on Helen's cheek and said goodbye.

Walking out into the bright sunshine did not make him feel any better. He could have understood if Helen couldn't be with him because he had let her down. It hurt so much, but he had to accept the fact that Helen still loved her husband. It had to be love. After all he had done to Helen, she loved him enough to take him home.

As Jerry paid the taxi driver, he looked around the garden. Things looked different now as he made his way up the path. Letting himself in, he threw the keys on the nearest table and glanced around. He loved Helen so much, but she didn't want to be with him. There were too many memories for him here now. He would call the estate agents. It was time to move on.

Helen was just lying there. She could not believe, after everything, that this doctor wanted her to take Mark home. She was so shocked by the remark that she could not reply and then Jerry suddenly got up and left. She wondered if he would come back. The next few days passed slowly. The nights were even longer as Mark and the events of the last few days haunted her dreams. Helen pulled herself out of bed and put on a loose fitting skirt; she found it too painful for trousers. She brushed her hair, swept it into a ponytail and was sitting beside the bed. Her parents had been permanent visitors the last four days. Jerry had not returned to see her; he hadn't even tried to contact her. Helen didn't try to contact him either. She couldn't deal with any more sorrow. There was a knock at the door, interrupting her thoughts.

"Come in." She couldn't hide the disappointment on her face as the nurse popped her head around the door.

"Your parents are here to take you home." She smiled warmly at Helen.

"Thanks, nurse, have there been any calls for me?" She could only hope.

"No, not today. I'll be back in a jiffy with your medicine."

Helen's burns were healing well. The doctors agreed that she could go home, as long as there was someone to care for her. Her parents were anxious, they wanted to make amends to their daughter. They, too, were filled with guilt and were delighted that she agreed to return to London with them. They loved her dearly. She had seen and heard nothing of Jerry all this time. In the ambulance he'd said he loved her. She resigned herself to the fact that he wasn't coming back, no matter how much she loved him.

Helen stepped out of the hospital into her parents' car, not looking forward to the long drive back to London. "Helen love, we thought you'd be comfy in the back seat where you could stretch out. Dad even brought some pillows, to help with the journey." Jessie held the door open for her daughter.

"Stop fussing, Mum. I'll be fine, honest."

Jessie settled Helen into the back seat before kissing her on the cheek. She said, "It'll be nice to have you home, Helen." She began sorting the pillows behind Helen.

"It'll be nice to be home, Mum." She winced as her leg brushed against the seat. At least she had painkillers for the journey, but that wouldn't stop her heart from aching. Her parents had left Louise with an auntie, and Helen was looking forward to seeing her daughter again. They had been apart too long. Now they would have to rebuild their life without Jerry.

Thirty

Helen was pacing back and forth. It had been four years since she left the hospital with her parents.

Mark was never prosecuted for his crimes. The authorities felt that a prison sentence would be futile. Mr Banes lost his licence and served six months for reckless driving. Constable Brown was now Sergeant Brown. Campbell was discharged from the police force. Dave Brown stayed in contact with Helen. She liked him and for the last eighteen months she had seen a lot of him. The burns had healed well. It had taken a long time for the emotional scars to heal. Even now they bothered her, but they were becoming easier to deal with.

A wave of pain ran across her stomach, making her gasp.

The pains were stronger now and the contractions were only three minutes apart. *Where's the bloody ambulance?* She remembered to call the college so Louise would meet her at the hospital. Why of all days did he have to be away today? She'd known that the moment he left the baby would come. At least it was only two weeks early and they were prepared for their new arrival. There was a knock at the door: just moments after her waters broke.

Louise was waiting at the hospital, but there was no time to talk with her mum as they took her straight to the labour suite. Louise made her way to the phone box.

"Hello, it's Louise. I think you should come home. Mum's having the baby!"

"Is Helen okay?" His voice was thick with emotion.

"Yes, she's in the labour suite now." Louise knew he hadn't wanted to go away, but Mum had insisted that he go on the training course. She'd promised him that she would be fine.

"I'll be on the next available flight. Thanks for calling me, Louise. See you soon."

She knew he might not get here until tomorrow, but at least he would come home. Louise paced back and forth until a kind nurse led her into a room. Mum looked tired and as she went closer she could see that she was holding the baby. Helen smiled when Louise came in.

"Come and meet your little brother," she said, smiling.

Louise kept her distance. "He's so small," she said. For six hours she had waited in the corridor. How could such a tiny thing take so long to be born?

"And like you, Louise, he's perfect." Helen smiled. She beckoned her daughter nearer. Louise carefully settled on the edge of the bed. Leaning over she whispered gently, "Hello there, little brother." She held his tiny hand. She was nervous. He looked so fragile that he might break.

Helen stared down at her new son. How life had moved on. She thought she could never be happy again after Mark, but she was. This little bundle would never know the pain that she and Louise had been through. Her son had a real family to love him. He would come home to a house of love, not hate. The baby made a noise, bringing Helen out of her thoughts.

The door opened. At first all Helen could see was a huge bouquet of flowers. By the size of it, it was every flower the shop had.

"Delivery for a new mum." He placed the flowers on the bed and wrapped his arms round Helen and kissed her passionately. Louise smiled as she left the room. Happy in the knowledge that they were a real family and life was good.

"I love you, Helen," he said, beaming at her. She looked tired, but her beauty was radiant.

"I love you too, Jerry." There was a pink flush appearing across her cheeks, aware of Louise's discreet exit.

He looked now at this tiny baby. He had Helen and now a son. He was overwhelmed. "What are we going to call this little fellow, then?" he asked as he held one of his tiny hands.

"What else but David?"

There was no other name. Jerry remembered sitting in the pub, every day for weeks, drowning his sorrows. This particular evening, though, Dave Brown arrived.

"So, this is what you're doing with yourself these days?"

Jerry didn't even look at Brown.

"Is it helping, then?"

Jerry ignored him but Dave wasn't going to let it go. He had seen Helen and she was just as miserable. They should be together and Dave was going to nudge them in the right direction.

"What are you doing, Jerry, how could you let her go like that?"

Jerry looked up from his pint.

"Hello to you too, Dave." The last thing he wanted was a lecture.

Dave sat down. "Are you just going to sit there feeling sorry for yourself, then?"

"Go away, Dave, I'm not in the mood."

"What happened between you two that you let her go after everything you both went through?" Jerry looked at Dave. It was obvious he wasn't leaving without some answers.

"She went back to that mongrel, Mark," he said through gritted teeth.

"No she didn't, mate; last time I looked he was still in the hospital, without Helen."

Jerry just stared as if he had been slapped in the face. "She left him at the hospital? Are you sure?"

"Yip, I spoke to Helen the other day and she has no intention of ever seeing Mark again."

It was then that Dave told him she had gone to her parents and, without a second thought, left Mark in the hospital. Dave gave Jerry Helen's phone number.

"Hello, Helen? It's Jerry, please don't hang up." There was a long silence before Helen recovered herself enough to speak

"Jerry, it's good to hear your voice."

"And yours too. Look, I'm sorry I keep making such a mess of things. I keep getting things all wrong, can you forgive me?"

"That depends on whether you keep making assumptions about me and what I think."

"Can we start over?"

"I don't know. I can't talk now. I'm meeting Louise and I'm late. Why don't you call me again and maybe we can talk?"

Jerry agreed, grateful that she had spoken to him instead of hanging up.

After a few telephone calls, Jerry went to London. He sold his cottage and purchased a flat nearby. It wasn't long until she and Louise moved in with him.

Dave Brown travelled on numerous occasions to see them, but for the last eighteen months it seemed he was a permanent lodger. Any time off he had was spent at their flat. Linda next door caught his attention and now romance was in full bloom.

There was just one more thing on Jerry's mind. It had been there since first coming to London to be with Helen. For nearly four years now he had been carrying around this ring in his pocket, waiting for the right moment, and now it was here.

"Helen, let's make our life complete." He hesitated before asking, "Will you marry me?"

She looked at him. They had been through a lot. She still had nightmares about her last meeting with Mark and, even though they had come a long way, sometimes she would find herself looking over her shoulder. There was no doubt in her mind that Jerry loved her, and it was real love, not the kind that Mark spoke of. There was only one answer she could give.

"Yes, I will." And with that, he kissed her deeply, tenderly and lovingly.